当当网终身五星级童书

★ ★ ★ ★ ★

我去找回太阳

[法] 克利斯提昂·约里波瓦 / 文　　　[法] 克利斯提昂·艾利施 / 图

郑迪蔚 / 译

二十一世纪出版社
21st Century Publishing House
全国百佳出版社

克利斯提昂·约里波瓦(Christian Jolibois)今年有 352 岁啦,他的妈妈是爱尔兰仙女,这可是个秘密哦。他可以不知疲倦地编出一串接一串异想天开的故事来。为了专心致志地写故事,他暂时把自己的"泰诺号"三桅船停靠在了勃艮第的一个小村庄旁边。并且,他还常常和猪、大树、玫瑰花和鸡在一块儿聊天。

克利斯提昂·艾利施(Christian Heinrich)像一只勤奋的小鸟,是个喜欢到处涂涂抹抹的水彩画家。他有一大把看起来很酷的秃头画笔,还带着自己小小的素描本去过许多没人知道的地方。他如今在斯特拉斯堡工作,整天幻想着去海边和鸬鹚聊天。

获奖记录:
2001年法国瑟堡青少年图书大奖
2003年法国高柯儿童文学大奖
2003年法国乡村儿童文学大奖
2006年法国阿弗尔儿童文学评审团奖

copyright 2003. by Editions Pocket Jeunesse, département d'Univers Poche − Paris,France.
Édition originale: NOM D'UNE POULE, ON A VOLE LE SOLEIL!

版权合同登记号 14-2006-023
Chinese simplified translation rights arranged with Univers Poche through Middle Kingdom Media.
本书中文版权通过法国文化出版传媒有限公司帮助获得。

图书在版编目(CIP)数据

我去找回太阳 / (法)约里波瓦著;
(法)艾利施绘;郑迪蔚译.
-南昌:二十一世纪出版社,2006.8(2011.10重印)
(不一样的卡梅拉)
ISBN 978-7-5391-3515-1

Ⅰ.我... Ⅱ.①约...②艾...③郑...
Ⅲ.图画故事-法国-现代 Ⅳ.I565.85

中国版本图书馆 CIP 数据核字(2006)第 100212 号

我去找回太阳

作 者	(法)克利斯提昂·约里波瓦 / 文
	(法)克利斯提昂·艾利施 / 图
译 者	郑迪蔚
责任编辑	熊 炽 张海虹
出版发行	二十一世纪出版社
	www.21cccc.com cc21@163.net
出 版 人	张秋林
印 刷	北京尚唐印刷包装有限公司
版 次	2006年9月第1版 2011年10月第30次印刷
开 本	600mm×940mm 1/32
印 张	1.5
书 号	ISBN 978-7-5391-3515-1
定 价	6.80 元

本社地址:江西省南昌市子安路 75 号 330009 (如发现印装质量问题,请寄本社图书发行公司调换 0791-6524997)

献给我正在新格里多尼亚岛上晒太阳的妹妹,欧迪勒和阿涅斯。

——克利斯提昂·约里波瓦

致我家乡的"向日葵"——小妹妹弗洛昂斯。

——克利斯提昂·艾利施

早上，太阳还没升起来，小公鸡和小母鸡们就已经醒了。

小六子、小胖墩、鼻涕虫、小刺头、娇气包……憋足了劲齐声喊："1，2，3！冲啊！"

小鸡们嘻嘻哈哈一齐冲进爸爸、妈妈温暖的被窝。

"喂,喂！爸爸、妈妈！给我们让个位子！"
"呀,这里真暖和呀！"

早上的撒娇可真够热闹的！

卡门和卡梅利多也钻进卡梅拉的怀里，"嗯，妈妈也给我让个位子呀！"

　　卡梅拉让开热被窝，将他们搂在翅膀下面，就像小时候一样。

爸爸皮迪克早就开始了每天的工作——叫醒太阳。

　　卡门趴在窗户上，崇拜地望着站在草垛顶上的父亲："爸爸，你太伟大了！"
　　皮迪克庄重地仰着头，他的嗓音既高亢又浑厚，还圆润、有力。

喔喔喔喔喔喔！

啊,奇迹出现了!

一轮红日随着皮迪克的打鸣声,
从天边冉冉升起。

爸爸,爸爸!

太阳，是我爸爸叫醒的！

"等我长大了，我也要指挥太阳！"卡门说。

"胡说八道！"小胖墩嘲笑道，"别忘了你是一个小女生！只有公鸡才能让太阳升起来！"

第二天,天空布满了乌云。

无论皮迪克怎么努力,也没能把太阳叫醒……更糟的是,还下起了大雨。

"别担心,爸爸! 你会成功的!"

几个小时过去了，几天过去了……太阳就好像聋了一样。

连续两个星期，都不见太阳的踪影。

6月18日这天，皮迪克还照常啼鸣，他用世界上所有的语言呼唤太阳——

英语：cook-a-doodle!

西班牙语：QUIQUIRIKI

俄语：KOU-KA-RÉ-KOU!

汉语：喔喔!

到了月底，还是见
不到太阳……

暴雨依旧下个不停……

17

"佩罗，你最有学问，快想想办法吧！这样下去怎么办呀？"卡门和卡梅利多把希望都寄托在佩罗身上了。

"你们要知道，我的孩子！"佩罗解释道，"太阳其实是天上的一个巨大无边的蛋黄……"

"当我们看不到它的时候……
那是它已经煮熟了！"

"佩罗变成老糊涂了！所有人都知道，太阳是
一个用煤气燃烧的大火球。"小卡门很失望。

鸡舍里正在策划一场阴谋政变：

"皮迪克老啦，他不行了！"小胖墩宣布说，"顶替他的时候到了。"

"对，说得对，不行就下来！"

"走！我们这就去草垛那儿把他轰下来！"

"伙伴们，我真的病了，我走不动。"鼻涕虫觉得外面冷，便找借口不去。

这天早上，皮迪克又失败了。
卡门和卡梅利多非常难过。

"快点！离开这里！快滚开！"

"让皮迪克先生看看我们的本事！"
"你们的爸爸已经老了！太阳还能听见老头的喊声吗？哈哈！"小胖墩嘲笑道。

"不许你这么说我爸爸！"卡梅利多愤怒地扑向小胖墩，他们在雨地里扭打了起来。

卡门最讨厌小公鸡们打架了，她拿起木棍，决定让这场争斗快点结束……

"卡门，如果不是你插手，我就被⋯⋯"

"嘿嘿，幸好没把你的嘴打歪。"
"喂，贝里奥，咱们一起去找太阳吧！"

"你们俩等我一下，我马上就回来。"

咔嚓！

"向日葵，听听这名字就知道，它的脑袋总是朝着太阳的。我们只要跟着这朵花指出的方向，就一定能找到太阳！"

"贝里奥，真没想到，我这个妹妹，小小年纪就知道这么多事……"

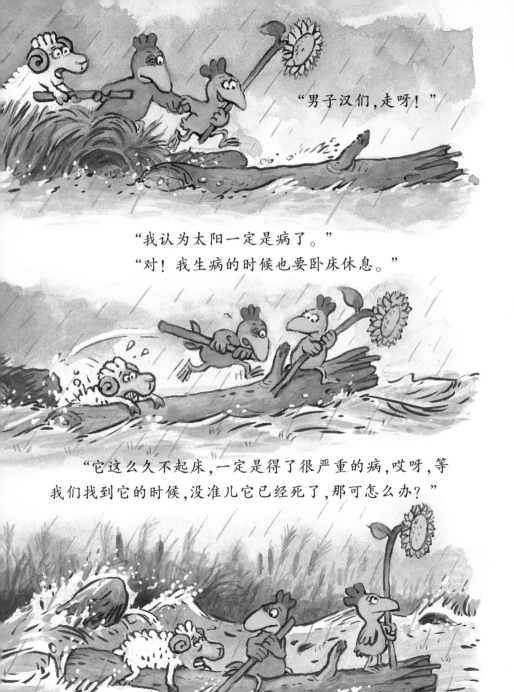

"男子汉们,走呀!"

"我认为太阳一定是病了。"
"对!我生病的时候也要卧床休息。"

"它这么久不起床,一定是得了很严重的病,哎呀,等我们找到它的时候,没准儿它已经死了,那可怎么办?"

天空还是阴雨绵绵。

在向日葵的指引下，贝里奥、卡门和卡梅利多，
到处寻找太阳可能躲藏的地方：田野、草地、树林，
连小山洞也没放过……

直到有一天……

"快看！"卡门大喊着，"向日葵指向柯尔贝大磨坊！"

"你们好，朋友们！"正在唱歌玩耍的鸭子柯尔贝，热情地向三个冒险家打招呼。

"哇，持续了一个月的阴雨天！这是我们鸭子最快乐的日子。"

嘎嘎嘎！嘎嘎嘎！

"来吧，朋友们！我们一起唱歌跳舞吧！"

我在雨中唱歌······

雨中唱歌多快乐······

"对不起,柯尔贝,我们可没什么心思唱。"卡梅利多说。

"我们在寻找太阳。"

"如果明天还找不到太阳,爸爸就会失去他的工作!"

"太阳？太——阳！"柯尔贝突然想起了什么，"对，太阳它就在楼上！跟我来，我带你们去。"

"这是蒙特哥菲尔兄弟生产纸张的厂房。"

"要这么多纸做什么？"贝里奥问。

"用来写点鸡同鸭讲的话呗！"

他脑子进
水了吧！

他们尾随着柯尔贝，悄悄穿过蒙特哥菲尔兄弟的卧室。

"啊！糟了！工作室的门锁上了。"

"别慌,我们从这个小洞钻进去!"

"瞧!就在这儿。"柯尔贝神气地说,
"我没有骗你们吧。"

"原来太阳藏在这儿啦！"三个小伙伴赶紧奔向"受困的太阳"。

"啊！它还活着呢！瞧，它看见我们有多高兴！"

"来，咱们赶紧把太阳救出去！1、2、3……"

埃蒂安被嘈杂声吵醒："约瑟夫,有只小粉鸡正在偷你的发明！"

"一只小粉鸡！哦,是吗？埃蒂安,别胡思乱想了,快回去睡觉吧！我们明天还有很多事情要做呢。"

气球慢慢地膨胀，鼓得又大又圆，它缓缓地向天空升去，好壮观啊！

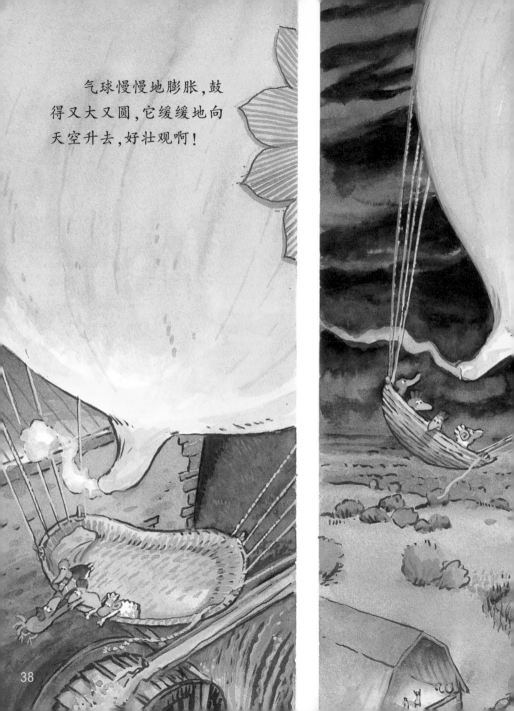

"太阳"带着小鸡、小鸭和小绵羊离开了陆地！
他们当然不知道，这是人类历史上第一次气
球载动物飞行！

"那些羊怎么会在天上呢？"贝里奥好奇地问。

"傻瓜，那是白云。"卡门说，"看这里，人们常说地球是圆的，看来是真的……"

看，我们的家！

　　鸡舍旁,卡梅拉陪着心情非常沉重的丈夫,去做最后一次尝试。

　　卡梅拉一再鼓励他要镇静,但皮迪克已经信心不足了,他颤巍巍地爬上草垛,满身大汗。

　　所有的鸡在雨中站成一排,这是皮迪克的最后一次机会。

　　"切! 他不会成功的!"有人幸灾乐祸地预测。

在一片寂静中，皮迪克用尽平生之力，
昂首向天空发出一声鸣叫。

太阳出来了！我成功了！！

啊!! 哎哟……

……这时,真正的太阳也升了起来。

这是个阳光明媚的早晨。

生活真美好啊！皮迪克抱起他的两个宝贝，美滋滋地往回走，造反的小公鸡们，灰溜溜地在一旁生闷气。

一个月来，太阳一直照耀着鸡舍，小鸡们又找回了生活中的乐趣。

卡门还发明了一个有趣的找太阳游戏：

1······2······3······看太阳！

而蒙特哥菲尔兄弟俩天天都在没完没了地争吵：

　　"约瑟夫，我发誓，当时告诉过你有只小粉鸡，还有一只绵羊和一只鸭子……"

"别找借口了，埃蒂安，用力打气！"

The Last Book of Wonder

ONE HOUSE ON THE PINNACLE LOOKING OVER THE EDGE OF THE WORLD

The Last
Book of Wonder

By
EDWARD JOHN M. D. P. DUNSANY
(LORD DUNSANY)

With Illustrations by
S. H. SIME

Short Story Index Reprint Series

BOOKS FOR LIBRARIES PRESS
FREEPORT, NEW YORK

First Published 1916
Reprinted 1969

STANDARD BOOK NUMBER:
8369-3219-6

LIBRARY OF CONGRESS CATALOG CARD NUMBER:
76-101282

MANUFACTURED
BY
HALLMARK LITHOGRAPHERS, INC.
IN THE U.S.A.

Preface

Ebrington Barracks
Aug. 16th 1916.

I do not know where I may be when this preface is read. As I write it in August 1916, I am at Ebrington Barracks, Londonderry, recovering from a slight wound. But it does not greatly matter where I am; my dreams are here before you amongst the following pages; and writing in a day when life is cheap, dreams seem to me all the dearer, the only things that survive.

Just now the civilization of Europe seems almost to have ceased, and nothing seems to grow in her torn fields but death, yet this is only for a while and dreams will come back again and bloom as of old, all the more radiantly for this terrible ploughing, as the flowers will bloom again where the trenches are and the primroses shelter in shell-holes for many seasons, when weeping Liberty has come home to Flanders.

To some of you in America this may seem an unnecessary and wasteful quarrel, as other people's quarrels often are; but it comes to this that though we are all killed there will be songs again, but if we were to submit and so survive there could be neither songs nor dreams, nor any joyous free things any more.

And do not regret the lives that are wasted amongst us, or the work that the dead would have done, for war is no accident that man's care could have averted, but is as natural, though not as regular, as the tides; as well regret the things that the tide has washed away, which destroys and cleanses and crumbles, and spares the minutest shells.

Preface

And now I will write nothing further about our war, but offer you these books of dreams from Europe as one throws things of value, if only to oneself, at the last moment out of a burning house.

Dunsany.

Contents

List of Illustrations

A Tale of London

"Come," said the Sultan to his hasheesh-eater in the very furthest lands that know Bagdad, "dream to me now of London."

And the hasheesh-eater made a low obeisance and seated himself cross-legged upon a purple cushion broidered with golden poppies, on the floor, beside an ivory bowl where the hasheesh was, and having eaten liberally of the hasheesh blinked seven times and spoke thus:

"O Friend of God, know then that London is the desiderate town even of all Earth's cities. Its houses are of ebony and cedar which they roof with thin copper plates that the hand of Time turns green. They have golden balconies in which amethysts are where they sit and watch the sunset. Musicians in the gloaming steal softly along the ways; unheard their feet fall on the white sea-sand with which those ways are strewn, and in the darkness suddenly they play on dulcimers and instruments with strings. Then are there murmurs in the balconies praising their skill, then are there bracelets cast down to them for reward and golden necklaces and even pearls.

"Indeed but the city is fair; there is by the sandy ways a paving all alabaster, and the lanterns along it are of chrysoprase, all night long they shine green, but of amethyst are the lanterns of the balconies.

"As the musicians go along the ways dancers gather about them and dance upon the alabaster pavings, for joy and not for hire. Sometimes a window opens far up in an ebony palace and a wreath is cast down to a dancer or orchids showered upon them.

"Indeed of many cities have I dreamt but of none fairer, through many marble metropolitan gates hasheesh has led me, but London is its secret, the last gate of all; the ivory bowl has nothing more to show. And indeed even now the imps that crawl behind me and that will not let me be are

2

plucking me by the elbow and bidding my spirit return, for well they know that I have seen too much. 'No, not London,' they say; and therefore I will speak of some other city, a city of some less mysterious land, and anger not the imps with forbidden things. I will speak of Persepolis or famous Thebes."

A shade of annoyance crossed the Sultan's face, a look of thunder that you had scarcely seen, but in those lands they watched his visage well, and though his spirit was wandering far away and his eyes were bleared with hasheesh yet that storyteller there and then perceived the look that was death, and sent his spirit back at once to London as a man runs into his house when the thunder comes.

"And therefore," he continued, "in the desiderate city, in London, all their camels are pure white. Remarkable is the swiftness of their horses, that draw their chariots that are of ivory along those sandy ways and that are of surpassing lightness, they have little bells of silver upon their horses' heads. O Friend of God, if you perceived their merchants! The glory of their dresses in the noonday! They are no less gorgeous than those butterflies that float about their streets. They have overcloaks of green and vestments of azure, huge purple flowers blaze on their overcloaks, the work of cunning needles, the centres of the flowers are of gold and the petals of purple. All their hats are black —" ("No, no," said the Sultan) —"but irises are set about the brims, and green plumes float above the crowns of them.

"They have a river that is named the Thames, on it their ships go up with violet sails bringing incense for the braziers that perfume the streets, new songs exchanged for gold with alien tribes, raw silver for the statues of their heroes, gold to make balconies where their women sit, great apphires to reward their poets with, the ecrets of old cities and strange lands, the earning of the dwellers in far isles, emeralds, diamonds and the hoards of the sea. And whenever a ship comes into port and furls its violet sails and the news spreads through London that she has come, then all the merchants go down to the river to barter, and all day long the chariots whirl through

4

the streets, and the sound of their going is a mighty roar all day until evening, their roar is even like —"

"Not so," said the Sultan.

"Truth is not hidden from the Friend of God," replied the hasheesh-eater, "I have erred being drunken with hasheesh, for in the desiderate city, even in London, so thick upon the ways is the white sea-sand with which the city glimmers that no sound comes from the path of the charioteers, but they go softly like a light sea-wind." ("It is well," said the Sultan.) "They go softly down to the port where the vessels are, and the merchandise in from the sea, amongst the wonders that the sailors show, on land by the high ships, and softly they go though swiftly at evening back to their homes.

"O would that the Munificent, the Illustrious, the Friend of God, had even seen these things, had seen the jewellers with their empty baskets, bargaining there by the ships, when the barrels of emeralds came up from the hold. Or would that he had seen the fountains there in silver basins in the midst of the ways. I have

seen small spires upon their ebony houses
and the spires were all of gold, birds strutted
there upon the copper roofs from golden
spire to spire that have no equal for splendour in all the woods of the world. And
over London the desiderate city the sky
is so deep a blue that by this alone the
traveller may know where he has come,
and may end his fortunate journey. Nor
yet for any colour of the sky is there too
great heat in London, for along its ways a
wind blows always from the South gently
and cools the city.

"Such, O Friend of God, is indeed the city
of London, lying very far off on the yonder
side of Bagdad, without a peer for beauty
or excellence of its ways among all the
towns of the earth or cities of song; and
even so, as I have told, its fortunate citizens dwell, with their hearts ever devising
beautiful things and from the beauty of
their own fair work that is more abundant
around them every year, receiving new
inspirations to work things more beautiful
yet."

"And is their government good?" the
Sultan said.

"It is most good," said the hasheesh-eater, and fell backwards upon the floor.

He lay thus and was silent. And when the Sultan perceived he would speak no more that night he smiled and lightly applauded.

And there was envy in that palace, in lands beyond Bagdad, of all that dwell in London.

Thirteen at Table

I n front of a spacious fireplace of the old kind, when the logs were well alight, and men with pipes and glasses were gathered before it in great easeful chairs, and the wild weather outside and the comfort that was within, and the season of the year — for it was Christmas — and the hour of the night, all called for the weird or uncanny, then out spoke the ex-master of foxhounds and told this tale.

I once had an odd experience too. It was when I had the Bromley and Sydenham, the year I gave them up — as a matter of fact it was the last day of the season. It was no use going on because there were no foxes left in the county, and London was sweeping down on us. You could see it from the kennels all along the skyline like a terrible army in grey, and masses of villas every year came skirmishing down our valleys. Our coverts were mostly on the hills, and as the town came down upon the valleys the foxes used to leave them and go right away out of the county and they never returned. I think they went by night and moved great distances. Well it was early April and we had drawn blank all day, and at the last draw of all, the very last of the season, we found a fox. He left the covert with his back to London and its railways and villas and wire and slipped away towards the chalk country and open Kent. I felt as I once felt as a child on one summer's day when I found a door in a garden where I played left luckily ajar, and I pushed it open and the wide lands were before me and waving fields of corn.

We settled down into a steady gallop and the fields began to drift by under us, and a great wind arose full of fresh breath. We left the clay lands where the bracken grows and came to a valley at the edge of the chalk. As we went down into it we saw the fox go up the other side like a shadow that crosses the evening, and glide into a wood that

9

stood on the top. We saw a flash of primroses in the wood and we were out the other
side, hounds hunting perfectly and the fox
still going absolutely straight. It began
to dawn on me then that we were in for a
great hunt, I took a deep breath when I
thought of it; the taste of the air of that
perfect Spring afternoon as it came to one
galloping, and the thought of a great run,
were together like some old rare wine.
Our faces now were to another valley, large
fields led down to it, with easy hedges, at
the bottom of it a bright blue stream went
singing and a rambling village smoked, the
sunlight on the opposite slopes danced like
a fairy; and all along the top old woods were
frowning, but they dreamed of Spring.
The "field" had fallen off and were far behind
and my only human companion was James,
my old first whip, who had a hound's in-
stinct, and a personal animosity against a
fox that even embittered his speech.

Across the valley the fox went as straight
as a railway line, and again we went without a check straight through the woods at
the top. I remember hearing men sing or
shout as they walked home from work, and

sometimes children whistled; the sounds came up from the village to the woods at the top of the valley. After that we saw no more villages, but valley after valley arose and fell before us as though we were voyaging some strange and stormy sea, and all the way before us the fox went dead up-wind like the fabulous Flying Dutchman. There was no one in sight now but my first whip and me, we had both of us got on to our second horses as we drew the last covert.

Two or three times we checked in those great lonely valleys beyond the village, but I began to have inspirations, I felt a strange certainty within me that this fox was going on straight up-wind till he died or until night came and we could hunt no longer, so I reversed ordinary methods and only cast straight ahead and always we picked up the scent again at once. I believe that this fox was the last one left in the villa-haunted lands and that he was prepared to leave them for remote uplands far from men, that if we had come the following day he would not have been there, and that we just happened to hit off his journey.

Evening began to descend upon the

11

valleys, still the hounds drifted on, like the lazy but unresting shadows of clouds upon a summer's day, we heard a shepherd calling to his dog, we saw two maidens move towards a hidden farm, one of them singing softly; no other sounds, but ours, disturbed the leisure and the loneliness of haunts that seemed not yet to have known the inventions of steam and gun-powder (even as China, they say, in some of her furthest mountains does not yet know that she has fought Japan).

And now the day and our horses were wearing out, but that resolute fox held on. I began to work out the run and to wonder where we were. The last landmark I had ever seen before must have been over five miles back and from there to the start was at least ten miles more. If only we could kill! Then the sun set. I wondered what chance we had of killing our fox. I looked at James' face as he rode beside me. He did not seem to have lost any confidence, yet his horse was as tired as mine. It was a good clear twilight and the scent was as strong as ever, and the fences were easy enough, but those valleys were terribly

12

trying and they still rolled on and on. It looked as if the light would outlast all possible endurance both of the fox and the horses, if the scent held good and he did not go to ground, otherwise night would end it. For long we had seen no houses and no roads, only chalk slopes with the twilight on them, and here and there some sheep, and scattered copses darkening in the evening. At some moment I seemed to realise all at once that the light was spent and that darkness was hovering, I looked at James, he was solemnly shaking his head. Suddenly in a little wooded valley we saw climb over the oaks the red-brown gables of a queer old house, at that instant I saw the fox scarcely heading by fifty yards. We blundered through a wood into full sight of the house, but no avenue led up to it or even a path nor were there any signs of wheel-marks anywhere. Already lights shone here and there in windows. We were in a park, and a fine park, but unkempt beyond credibility; brambles grew everywhere. It was too dark to see the fox any more but we knew he was dead beat, the hounds were just before us,— and a four-foot railing of oak.

13

I shouldn't have tried it on a fresh horse at the beginning of a run, and here was a horse near his last gasp. But what a run! an event standing out in a lifetime, and the hounds close up on their fox, slipping into the darkness as I hesitated. I decided to try it. My horse rose about eight inches and took it fair with his breast, and the oak log flew into handfuls of wet decay — it was rotten with years. And then we were on a lawn and at the far end of it the hounds were tumbling over their fox. Fox, horses and light were all done together at the end of a twenty-mile point. We made some noise then, but nobody came out of the queer old house.

I felt pretty stiff as I walked round to the hall door with the mask and the brush while James went with the hounds and the two horses to look for the stables. I rang a bell marvellously encrusted with rust, and after a long while the door opened a little way revealing a hall with much old armour in it and the shabbiest butler that I have ever known.

I asked him who lived there. Sir Richard Arlen. I explained that my horse

could go no further that night and that I
wished to ask Sir Richard Arlen for a bed
for the night.

"O, no one ever comes here, sir," said the
butler.

I pointed out that I had come.

"I don't think it would be possible, sir,"
he said.

This annoyed me and I asked to see Sir
Richard, and insisted until he came. Then
I apologised and explained the situation.
He looked only fifty, but a 'Varsity oar on
the wall with the date of the early seventies,
made him older than that; his face had
something of the shy look of the hermit;
he regretted that he had not room to put
me up. I was sure that this was untrue,
also I had to be put up there, there was nowhere else within miles, so I almost insisted.
Then to my astonishment he turned to the
butler and they talked it over in an under-
tone. At last they seemed to think that
they could manage it, though clearly with
reluctance. It was by now seven o'clock and
Sir Richard told me he dined at half past
seven. There was no question of clothes
for me other than those I stood in, as my

host was shorter and broader. He showed me presently to the drawing-room and there he reappeared before half past seven in evening dress and a white waistcoat. The drawing-room was large and contained old furniture but it was rather worn than venerable, an Aubusson carpet flapped about the floor, the wind seemed momently to enter the room, and old draughts haunted corners; the stealthy feet of rats that were never at rest indicated the extent of the ruin that time had wrought in the wainscot; somewhere far off a shutter flapped to and fro, the guttering candles were insufficient to light so large a room. The gloom that these things suggested was quite in keeping with Sir Richard's first remark to me after he entered the room: "I must tell you, sir, that I have led a wicked life. O, a very wicked life."

Such confidences from a man much older than oneself after one has known him for half an hour are so rare that any possible answer merely does not suggest itself. I said rather slowly, "O, really," and chiefly to forestall another such remark I said, "What a charming house you have."

"Yes," he said, "I have not left it for nearly forty years. Since I left the 'Varsity. One is young there, you know, and one has opportunities; but I make no excuses, no excuses." And the door slipping its rusty latch, came drifting on the draught into the room, and the long carpet flapped and the hangings upon the walls, then the draught fell rustling away and the door slammed to again.

"Ah, Marianne," he said, "we have a guest to-night. Mr. Linton. This is Marianne Gib." And everything became clear to me. "Mad," I said to myself, for no one had entered the room.

The rats ran up the length of the room behind the wainscot ceaselessly, and the wind unlatched the door again and the folds of the carpet fluttered up to our feet and stopped there, for our weight held it down.

"Let me introduce Mr. Linton," said my host — "Lady Mary Errinjer."

The door slammed back again. I bowed politely. Even had I been invited I should have humoured him, but it was the very least that an uninvited guest could do.

This kind of thing happened eleven times,

the rustling, and the fluttering of the carpet, and the footsteps of the rats, and the restless door, and then the sad voice of my host introducing me to phantoms. Then for some while we waited while I struggled with the situation; conversation flowed slowly. And again the draught came trailing up the room, while the flaring candles filled it with hurrying shadows. "Ah, late again, Cicely," said my host in his soft, mournful way. "Always late, Cicely." Then I went down to dinner with that man and his mind and the twelve phantoms that haunted it. I found a long table with fine old silver on it and places laid for fourteen. The butler was now in evening dress, there were fewer draughts in the dining-room, the scene was less gloomy there. "Will you sit next to Rosalind at the other end," Sir Richard said to me. "She always takes the head of the table, I wronged her most of all." I said, "I shall be delighted."

I looked at the butler closely, but never did I see by any expression of his face or by anything that he did any suggestion that he waited upon less than fourteen people in the complete possession of all their faculties.

Perhaps a dish appeared to be refused more often than taken but every glass was equally filled with champagne. At first I found little to say, but when Sir Richard speaking from the far end of the table said, "You are tired, Mr. Linton," I was reminded that I owed something to a host upon whom I had forced myself. It was excellent champagne and with the help of a second glass I made the effort to begin a conversation with a Miss Helen Errold for whom the place upon one side of me was laid. It came more easy to me very soon, I frequently paused in my monologue, like Mark Anthony, for a reply, and sometimes I turned and spoke to Miss Rosalind Smith. Sir Richard at the other end talked sorrowfully on, he spoke as a condemned man might speak to his judge, and yet somewhat as a judge might speak to one that he once condemned wrongly. My own mind began to turn to mournful things. I drank another glass of champagne, but I was still thirsty. I felt as if all the moisture in my body had been blown away over the downs of Kent by the wind up which we had galloped. Still I was not talking enough; my host was looking at me. I made another effort, after all I had something to talk about, a twenty-mile point is not often seen in a lifetime, especially south of the Thames. I began to describe the run to Rosalind Smith. I could see then that my host was pleased, the sad look in his face gave a kind of a flicker, like mist upon the mountains on a miserable day when a faint puff comes from the sea and the mist would lift if it could. And the butler refilled my glass very attentively. I asked her first if she hunted, and paused and began my story. I told her where we had found the fox and how fast and straight he had gone, and how I had got through the village by keeping to the road, while the little gardens and wire, and then the river, had stopped the rest of the field. I told her the kind of country that we crossed and how splendid it looked in the Spring, and how mysterious the valleys were as soon as the twilight came, and what a glorious horse I had and how wonderfully he went. I was so fearfully thirsty after the great hunt that I had to stop for a moment now and then, but I went on with my descrip-

tion of that famous run, for I had warmed
to the subject, and after all there was
nobody to tell of it but me except my old
whipper-in, and "the old fellow's probably
drunk by now," I thought. I described to
her minutely the exact spot in the run at
which it had come to me clearly that this
was going to be the greatest hunt in the
whole history of Kent. Sometimes I forgot incidents that had happened as one
well may in a run of twenty miles, and
then I had to fill in the gaps by inventing.
I was pleased to be able to make the party
go off well by means of my conversation,
and besides that the lady to whom I was
speaking was extremely pretty: I do not
mean in a flesh and blood kind of way but
there were little shadowy lines about the
chair beside me that hinted at an unusually
graceful figure when Miss Rosalind Smith
was alive; and I began to perceive that
what I first mistook for the smoke of guttering candles and a table-cloth waving in
the draught was in reality an extremely
animated company who listened, and not
without interest, to my story of by far the
greatest hunt that the world had ever

known: indeed I told them that I would
confidently go further and predict that
never in the history of the world would there
be such a run again. Only my throat was
terribly dry. And then as it seemed they
wanted to hear more about my horse. I
had forgotten that I had come there on a
horse, but when they reminded me it all
came back; they looked so charming leaning over the table intent upon what I said,
that I told them everything they wanted
to know. Everything was going so pleasantly if only Sir Richard would cheer up.
I heard his mournful voice every now and
then — these were very pleasant people
if only he would take them the right way.
I could understand that he regretted his
past, but the early seventies seemed centuries away and I felt sure that he misunder-
stood these ladies, they were not revenge-
ful as he seemed to suppose. I wanted to
show him how cheerful they really were,
and so I made a joke and they all laughed
at it, and then I chaffed them a bit, especially Rosalind, and nobody resented it in
the very least. And still Sir Richard sat
there with that unhappy look, like one that

has ended weeping because it is vain and has not the consolation even of tears.

We had been a long time there and many of the candles had burned out, but there was light enough. I was glad to have an audience for my exploit, and being happy myself I was determined Sir Richard should be. I made more jokes and they still laughed good-naturedly; some of the jokes were a little broad perhaps but no harm was meant. And then — I do not wish to excuse myself— but I had had a harder day than I ever had had before and without knowing it I must have been completely exhausted; in this state the champagne had found me, and what would have been harmless at any other time must somehow have got the better of me when quite tired out — anyhow I went too far, I made some joke — I cannot in the least remember what — that suddenly seemed to offend them. I felt all at once a commotion in the air, I looked up and saw that they had all arisen from the table and were sweeping towards the door: I had not time to open it but it blew open on a wind, I could scarcely see what Sir Richard was doing because

23

only two candles were left, I think the rest blew out when the ladies suddenly rose. I sprang up to apologise, to assure them — and then fatigue overcame me as it had overcome my horse at the last fence, I clutched at the table but the cloth came away and then I fell. The fall, and the darkness on the floor and the pent up fatigue of the day overcame me all three together.

The sun shone over glittering fields and in at a bedroom window and thousands of birds were chanting to the Spring, and there I was in an old four-poster bed in a quaint old panelled bedroom, fully dressed and wearing long muddy boots; someone had taken my spurs and that was all. For a moment I failed to realise and then it all came back, my enormity and the pressing need of an abject apology to Sir Richard. I pulled an embroidered bell rope until the butler came. He came in perfectly cheerful and indescribably shabby. I asked him if Sir Richard was up, and he said he had just gone down, and told me to my amazement that it was twelve o'clock. I asked to be shown in to Sir Richard at once. He was in his

24

smoking-room. "Good morning," he said cheerfully the moment I went in. I went directly to the matter in hand. "I fear that I insulted some ladies in your house —" I began.

"You did indeed," he said, "You did indeed." And then he burst into tears and took me by the hand. "How can I ever thank you?" he said to me then. "We have been thirteen at table for thirty years and I never dared to insult them because I had wronged them all, and now you have done it and I know they will never dine here again." And for a long time he still held my hand, and then he gave it a grip and a kind of a shake which I took to mean "Good-bye" and I drew my hand away then and left the house. And I found James in the stables with the hounds and asked him how he had fared, and James, who is a man of very few words, said he could not rightly remember, and I got my spurs from the butler and climbed on to my horse and slowly we rode away from that queer old house, and slowly we wended home, for the hounds were footsore but happy and the horses were tired still. And when we recalled that the hunting season was ended we turned our faces to Spring and thought of the new things that try to replace the old. And that very year I heard, and have often heard since, of dances and happier dinners at Sir Richard Arlen's house.

The City on Mallington Moor

Besides the old shepherd at Lingwold whose habits render him unreliable I am probably the only person that has ever seen the city on Mallington Moor.

I had decided one year to do no London season; partly because of the ugliness of the things in the shops, partly because of the unresisted invasions of German bands, partly perhaps because some pet parrots in the oblong where I lived had learned to imitate cab-whistles; but chiefly because of late there had seized me in London a quite unreasonable longing for large woods and waste spaces, while the very thought of little valleys underneath copses full of bracken and foxgloves was a torment to me and every summer in London the longing

grew worse till the thing was becoming
intolerable. So I took a stick and a knap-
sack and began walking northwards, starting at Tetherington and sleeping at inns,
where one could get real salt, and the waiter
spoke English and where one had a name
instead of a number; and though the table-
cloth might be dirty the windows opened
so that the air was clean, where one had the
excellent company of farmers and men of
the wold, who could not be thoroughly
vulgar, because they had not the money
to be so even if they had wished it. At
first the novelty was delightful, and then
one day in a queer old inn up Uthering
way, beyond Lingwold, I heard for the first
time the rumour of the city said to be on
Mallington Moor. They spoke of it quite
casually over their glasses of beer, two farmers at the inn. "They say the queer folk
be at Mallington with their city," one
farmer said. "Travelling they seem to be,"
said the other. And more came in then and
the rumour spread. And then, such are the
contradictions of our little likes and dislikes
and all the whims that drive us, that I, who
had come so far to avoid cities, had a great

longing all of a sudden for throngs again and the great hives of Man, and then and there determined on that bright Sunday morning to come to Mallington and there search for the city that rumour spoke of so strangely.

Mallington Moor, from all that they said of it, was hardly a likely place to find a thing by searching. It was a huge high moor, very bleak and desolate and altogether trackless. It seemed a lonely place from what they said. The Normans when they came had called it Mal Lieu and afterwards Mallintown and so it changed to Mallington. Though what a town can ever have had to do with a place so utterly desolate I do not know. And before that some say that the Saxons called it Baplas, which I believe to be a corruption of Bad Place.

And beyond the mere rumour of a beautiful city all of white marble and with a foreign look up on Mallington Moor, beyond this I could not get. None of them had seen it himself, "only heard of it like," and my questions, rather than stimulating conversation, would always stop it abruptly.

I was no more fortunate on the road to Mallington until the Tuesday, when I was quite near it; I had been walking two days from the inn where I had heard the rumour and could see the great hill steep as a headland on which Mallington lay, standing up on the skyline: the hill was covered with grass, where anything grew at all, but Mallington Moor is all heather; it is just marked Moor on the map; nobody goes there and they do not trouble to name it. It was there where the gaunt hill first came into sight, by the roadside as I enquired for the marble city of some labourers by the way, that I was directed, partly I think in derision, to the old shepherd of Lingwold. It appeared that he, following sometimes sheep that had strayed, and wandering far from Lingwold, came sometimes up to the edge of Mallington Moor, and that he would come back from these excursions and shout through the villages, raving of a city of white marble and gold-tipped minarets. And hearing me asking questions of this city they had laughed and directed me to the shepherd of Lingwold. One well-meant warning they gave me as I went — the old man was not reliable.

And late that evening I saw the thatches of Lingwold sheltering under the edge of that huge hill that Atlas-like held up those miles of moor to the great winds and heaven.

They knew less of the city in Lingwold than elsewhere but they knew the whereabouts of the man I wanted, though they seemed a little ashamed of him. There was an inn in Lingwold that gave me shelter, whence in the morning, equipped with purchases, I set out to find their shepherd. And there he was on the edge of Mallington Moor standing motionless, gazing stupidly at his sheep; his hands trembled continually and his eyes had a blear look, but he was quite sober, wherein all Lingwold had wronged him.

And then and there I asked him of the city and he said he had never heard tell of any such place. And I said, "Come, come, you must pull yourself together." And he looked angrily at me; but when he saw me draw from amongst my purchases a full bottle of whiskey and a big glass he became more friendly. As I poured out the whiskey I asked him again about the marble city on Mallington Moor but he seemed quite honestly to know nothing about it. The amount of whiskey he drank was quite incredible, but I seldom express surprise and once more I asked him the way to the wonderful city. His hand was steadier now and his eyes more intelligent and he said that he had heard something of some such city, but his memory was evidently blurred and he was still unable to give me useful directions. I consequently gave him another tumbler, which he drank off like the first without any water, and almost at once he was a different man. The trembling in his hands stopped altogether, his eye became as quick as a younger man's, he answered my questions readily and frankly, and, what was more important to me still, his old memory became alert and clear for even minutest details. His gratitude to myself I need not mention, for I make no pretence that I bought the bottle of whiskey that the old shepherd enjoyed so much without at least some thought of my own advantage. Yet it was pleasant to reflect that it was due to me that he had pulled himself together and steadied his shaking hand and cleared his mind, recovered his memory and his self-respect. He spoke to me quite clearly, no longer slurring his words; he had seen the city first one moonlight night when he was lost in the mist on the big moor, he had wandered far in the mist, and when it lifted he saw the city by moonlight. He had no food, but luckily had his flask. There never was such a city, not even in books. Travellers talked sometimes of Venice seen from the sea, there might be such a place or there might not, but, whether or no, it was nothing to the city on Mallington Moor. Men who read books had talked to him in his time, hundreds of books, but they never could tell of any city like this. Why, the place was all of marble, roads, walls and palaces, all pure white marble, and the tops of the tall thin spires were entirely of gold. And they were queer folk in the city even for foreigners. And there were camels, but I cut him short for I thought I could judge for myself, if there was such a place, and, if not, I was wasting my time as well as a pint of good whiskey. So I got him to speak of the way, and after more circumlocution than I needed and more talk of the city he pointed to a tiny track on the black earth just beside us, a little twisty way you could hardly see.

I said the moor was trackless; untrodden of man or dog it certainly was and seemed to have less to do with the ways of man than any waste I have seen, but the track the old shepherd showed me, if track it was, was no more than the track of a hare — an elf-path the old man called it, Heaven knows what he meant. And then before I left him he insisted on giving me his flask with the queer strong rum it contained. Whiskey brings out in some men melancholy, in some rejoicing, with him it was clearly generosity and he insisted until I took his rum, though I did not mean to drink it. It was lonely up there, he said, and bitter cold and the city hard to find, being set in a hollow, and I should need the rum, and he had never seen the marble city except on days when he had had his flask: he seemed to regard that rusted iron flask as a sort of mascot, and in the end I took it.

I followed that odd, faint track on the black earth under the heather till I came to the big grey stone beyond the horizon, where the track divides into two, and I took the one to the left as the old man told me. I knew by another stone that I saw far off that I had not lost my way, nor the old man lied.

And just as I hoped to see the city's ramparts before the gloaming fell on that desolate place, I suddenly saw a long high wall of whiteness with pinnacles here and there thrown up above it, floating towards me silent and grim as a secret, and knew it for that evil thing the mist. The sun, though low, was shining on every sprig of heather, the green and scarlet mosses were shining with it too, it seemed incredible that in three minutes' time all those colours would be gone and nothing left all round but a grey darkness. I gave up hope of finding the city that day, a broader path than mine could have been quite easily lost. I hastily chose for my bed a thick patch of heather, wrapped myself in a waterproof cloak, and lay down and made myself comfortable. And then the mist came. It came like the careful pulling of lace curtains, then like the drawing of grey blinds; it shut out the horizon to the north, then to the east and west;

35

it turned the whole sky white and hid the moor; it came down on it like a metropolis, only utterly silent, silent and white as tombstones.

And then I was glad of that strange strong rum, or whatever it was in the flask that the shepherd gave me, for I did not think that the mist would clear till night, and .I feared the night would be cold. So I nearly emptied the flask; and, sooner than I expected, I fell asleep, for the first night out as a rule one does not sleep at once but is kept awake some while by the little winds and the unfamiliar sound of the things that wander at night, and that cry to one another far-off with their queer, faint voices; one misses them afterwards when one gets to houses again. But I heard none of these sounds in the mist that evening.

And then I woke and found that the mist was gone and the sun was just disappearing under the moor, and I knew that I had not slept for as long as I thought. And I decided to go on while I could, for I thought that I was not very far from the city.

I went on and on along the twisty track, bits of the mist came down and filled the

36

hollows but lifted again at once so that I saw my way. The twilight faded as I went, a star appeared, and I was able to see the track no longer. I could go no further that night, yet before I lay down to sleep I decided to go and look over the edge of a wide depression in the moor that I saw a little way off. So I left the track and walked a few hundred yards, and when I got to the edge the hollow was full of mist all white underneath me. Another star appeared and a cold wind arose, and with the wind the mist flapped away like a curtain. And there was the city.

Nothing the shepherd had said was the least untrue or even exaggerated. The poor old man had told the simple truth, there is not a city like it in the world. What he had called thin spires were minarets, but the little domes on the top were clearly pure gold as he said. There were the marble terraces he described and the pure white palaces covered with carving and hundreds of minarets. The city was obviously of the East and yet where there should have been crescents on the domes of the minarets there were golden suns with rays, and

37

wherever one looked one saw things that obscured its origin. I walked down to it, and, passing through a wicket gate of gold in a low wall of white marble, I entered the city. The heather went right up to the city's edge and beat against the marble wall whenever the wind blew it. Lights began to twinkle from high windows of blue glass as I walked up the white street, beautiful copper lanterns were lit up and let down from balconies by silver chains, from doors ajar came the sound of voices singing, and then I saw the men. Their faces were rather grey than black, and they wore beautiful robes of coloured silk with hems embroidered with gold and some with copper, and sometimes pacing down the marble ways with golden baskets hung on each side of them I saw the camels of which the old shepherd spoke.

The people had kindly faces, but, though they were evidently friendly to strangers, I could not speak with them being ignorant of their language, nor were the sounds of the syllables they used like any language I had ever heard: they sounded more like grouse.

38

When I tried to ask them by signs whence they had come with their city they would only point to the moon, which was bright and full and was shining fiercely on those marble ways till the city danced in light. And now there began appearing one by one, slipping softly out through windows, men with stringed instruments in the balconies. They were strange instruments with huge bulbs of wood, and they played softly on them and very beautifully, and their queer voices softly sang to the music weird dirges of the griefs of their native land wherever that may be. And far off in the heart of the city others were singing too, the sound of it came to me wherever I roamed, not loud enough to disturb my thoughts, but gently turning the mind to pleasant things. Slender carved arches of marble, as delicate almost as lace, crossed and re-crossed the ways wherever I went. There was none of that hurry of which foolish cities boast, nothing ugly or sordid so far as I could see. I saw that it was a city of beauty and song. I wondered how they had travelled with all that marble, how they had laid it down on Mallington Moor, whence they had come and what their resources were, and determined to investigate closely next morning, for the old shepherd had not troubled his head to think how the city came, he had only noted that the city was there (and of course no one believed him, though that is partly his fault for his dissolute ways). But at night one can see little and I had walked all day, so I determined to find a place to rest in. And just as I was wondering whether to ask for shelter of those silk-robed men by signs or whether to sleep outside the walls and enter again in the morning, I came to a great archway in one of the marble houses with two black curtains, embroidered below with gold, hanging across it. Over the archway were carved apparently in many tongues the words: "Here strangers rest." In Greek, Latin and Spanish the sentence was repeated and there was writing also in the language that you see on the walls of the great temples of Egypt, and Arabic and what I took to be early Assyrian and one or two languages I had never seen. I entered through the curtains and found a tesselated marble court with golden braziers burning sleepy incense swinging by chains from the roof, all round the walls were comfortable mattresses lying upon the floor covered with cloths and silks. It must have been ten o'clock and I was tired. Outside the music still softly filled the streets, a man had set a lantern down on the marble way, five or six sat down round him, and he was sonorously telling them a story. Inside there were some already asleep on the beds, in the middle of the wide court under the braziers a woman dressed in blue was singing very gently, she did not move, but sung on and on, I never heard a song that was so soothing. I lay down on one of the mattresses by the wall, which was all inlaid with mosaics, and pulled over me some of the cloths with their beautiful alien work, and almost immediately my thoughts seemed part of the song that the woman was singing in the midst of the court under the golden braziers that hung from the high roof, and the song turned them to dreams, and so I fell asleep.

A small wind having arisen, I was awakened by a sprig of heather that beat continually against my face. It was morning on Mallington Moor, and the city was quite gone.

Why the Milkman Shudders
When he Perceives the Dawn

n the Hall of the Ancient Company of Milkmen round the great fireplace at the end, when the winter logs are burning and all the craft are assembled they tell to-day, as their grandfathers told before them, why the milkman shudders when he perceives the dawn.

When dawn comes creeping over the edges of hills, peers through the tree trunks making wonderful shadows, touches the tops of tall columns of smoke going up from awakening cottages in the valleys, and breaks all golden over Kentish fields, when going on tip-toe thence it comes to the walls of London and slips all shyly up those gloomy streets the milkman perceives it and shudders.

The Last Book of Wonder

A man may be a Milkman's Working Apprentice, may know what borax is and how to mix it, yet not for that is the story told to him. There are five men alone that tell that story, five men appointed by the Master of the Company, by whom each place is filled as it falls vacant, and if you do not hear it from one of them you hear the story from none and so can never know why the milkman shudders when he perceives the dawn.

It is the way of one of these five men, greybeards all and milkmen from infancy, to rub his hands by the fire when the great logs burn, and to settle himself more easily in his chair, perhaps to sip some drink far other than milk, then to look round to see that none are there to whom it would not be fitting the tale should be told and, looking from face to face and seeing none but the men of the Ancient Company, and questioning mutely the rest of the five with his eyes, if some of the five be there, and receiving their permission, to cough and to tell the tale. And a great hush falls in the Hall of the Ancient Company, and something about the shape of the roof and the rafters makes the tale resonant all down the hall so that the youngest hears it far away from the fire and knows, and dreams of the day when perhaps he will tell himself why the milkman shudders when he perceives the dawn.

Not as one tells some casual fact is it told, nor is it commented on from man to man, but it is told by that great fire only and when the occasion and the stillness of the room and the merit of the wine and the profit of all seem to warrant it in the opinion of the five deputed men: then does one of them tell it, as I have said, not heralded by any master of ceremonies but as though it arose out of the warmth of the fire before which his knotted hands would chance to be; not a thing learned by rote, but told differently by each teller, and differently according to his mood, yet never has one of them dared to alter its salient points, there is none so base among the Company of Milkmen. The Company of Powderers for the Face know of this story and have envied it, the Worthy Company of Chin-Barbers, and the Company of Whiskerers; but none have heard it in the Milkmen's

Hall, through whose wall no rumour of the secret goes, and though they have invented tales of their own Antiquity mocks them.

This mellow story was ripe with honourable years when milkmen wore beaver hats, its origin was still mysterious when white smocks were the vogue, men asked one another when Stuarts were on the throne (and only the Ancient Company knew the answer) why the milkman shudders when he perceives the dawn. It is all for envy of this tale's reputation that the Company of Powderers for the Face have invented the tale that they too tell of an evening, "Why the Dog Barks when he hears the step of the Baker"; and because probably all men know that tale the Company of Powderers for the Face have dared to consider it famous. Yet it lacks mystery and is not ancient, is not fortified with classical allusion, has no secret lore, is common to all who care for an idle tale, and shares with "The Wars of the Elves," the Calf-butcher's tale, and "The Story of the Unicorn and the Rose," which is the tale of the Company of Horse-drivers, their obvious inferiority.

But unlike all these tales so new to time, and many another that the last two centuries tell, the tale that the milkmen tell ripples wisely on, so full of quotation from the profoundest writers, so full of recondite allusion, so deeply tinged with all the wisdom of man and instructive with the experience of all times that they that hear it in the Milkmen's Hall as they interpret allusion after allusion and trace obscure quotation lose idle curiosity and forget to question why the milkman shudders when he perceives the dawn.

You also, O my reader, give not yourself up to curiosity. Consider of how many it is the bane. Would you to gratify this tear away the mystery from the Milkmen's Hall and wrong the Ancient Company of Milkmen? Would they if all the world knew it and it became a common thing tell that tale any more that they have told for the last four hundred years? Rather a silence would settle upon their hall and a universal regret for the ancient tale and the ancient winter evenings. And though curiosity were a proper consideration yet even then this is not the proper place nor this the

46

proper occasion for the Tale. For the proper place is only the Milkmen's Hall and the proper occasion only when logs burn well and when wine has been deeply drunken, then when the candles were burning well in long rows down to the dimness, down to the darkness and mystery that lie at the end of the hall, then were you one of the Company, and were I one of the five, would I rise from my seat by the fireside and tell you with all the embellishments that it has gleaned from the ages that story that is the heirloom of the milkmen. And the long candles would burn lower and lower and gutter and gutter away till they liquified in their sockets, and draughts would blow from the shadowy end of the hall stronger and stronger till the shadows came after them, and still I would hold you with that treasured story, not by any wit of mine but all for the sake of its glamour and the times out of which it came; one by one the candles would flare and die and, when all were gone, by the light of ominous sparks when each milkman's face looks fearful to his fellow, you would know, as now you cannot, why the milkman shudders when he perceives the dawn.

The Bad Old
Woman in Black

T he bad old woman in black ran down the street of the ox-butchers.

Windows at once were opened high up in those crazy gables; heads were thrust out: it was she. Then there arose the counsel of anxious voices, calling sideways from window to window or across to opposite houses. Why was she there with her sequins and bugles and old black gown? Why had she left her dreaded house? On what fell errand she hasted?

They watched her lean, lithe figure, and the wind in that old black dress, and soon she was gone from the cobbled street and under the town's high gateway. She turned at once to her right and was hid from the

48

THE BAD OLD WOMAN IN BLACK RAN DOWN THE STREET OF THE
OX-BUTCHERS

view of the houses. Then they all ran down to their doors, and small groups formed on the pavement; there they took counsel together, the eldest speaking first. Of what they had seen they said nothing, for there was no doubt it was she; it was of the future they spoke, and the future only.

In what notorious thing would her errand end? What gains had tempted her out from her fearful home? What brilliant but sinful scheme had her genius planned? Above all, what future evil did this portend? Thus at first it was only questions. And then the old grey-beards spoke, each one to a little group; they had seen her out before, had known her when she was younger, and had noted the evil things that had followed her goings: the small groups listened well to their low and earnest voices. No one asked questions now or guessed at her infamous errand, but listened only to the wise old men who knew the things that had been, and who told the younger men of the dooms that had come before.

Nobody knew how many times she had left her dreaded house; but the oldest recounted all the times that they knew, and the way she had gone each time, and the doom that had followed her going; and two could remember the earthquake that there was in the street of the shearers.

So were there many tales of the times that were, told on the pavement near the old green doors by the edge of the cobbled street, and the experience that the aged men had bought with their white hairs might be had cheap by the young. But from all their experience only this was clear, that never twice in their lives had she done the same infamous thing, and that the same calamity twice had never followed her goings. Therefore it seemed that means were doubtful and few for finding out what thing was about to befall; and an ominous feeling of gloom came down on the street of the ox-butchers. And in the gloom grew fears of the very worst. This comfort they only had when they put their fear into words — that the doom that followed her goings had never yet been anticipated. One feared that with magic she meant to move the moon; and he would have dammed the high tide on the neighbouring coast, knowing that as the moon attracted the sea

the sea must attract the moon, and hoping
by his device to humble her spells. Another would have fetched iron bars and
clamped them across the street, remember-
ing the earthquake there was in the street
of the shearers. Another would have honoured his household gods, the little cat-
faced idols seated above his hearth, gods to
whom magic was no unusual thing, and,
having paid their fees and honoured them
well, would have put the whole case before
them. His scheme found favour with many,
and yet at last was rejected, for others ran
indoors and brought out their gods too, to
be honoured, till there was a herd of gods
all seated there on the pavement; yet
would they have honoured them and put
their case before them but that a fat man
ran up last of all, carefully holding under a
reverent arm his own two hound-faced gods,
though he knew well — as, indeed, all men
must — that they were notoriously at war
with the little cat-faced idols. And although the animosities natural to faith had
all been lulled by the crisis, yet a look of
anger had come in the cat-like faces that no
one dared disregard, and all perceived that

if they stayed a moment longer there would be flaming around them the jealousy of the gods; so each man hastily took his idols home, leaving the fat man insisting that his hound-faced gods should be honoured.

Then were there schemes again and voices raised in debate, and many new dangers feared and new plans made.

But in the end they made no defence against danger, for they knew not what it would be, but wrote upon parchment as a warning and in order that all might know: *"The bad old woman in black ran down the street of the ox-butchers."*

The Bird of the Difficult Eye

Observant men and women that know their Bond Street well will appreciate my astonishment when in a jewellers' shop I perceived that nobody was furtively watching me. Not only this but when I even picked up a little carved crystal to examine it no shop-assistants crowded round me. I walked the whole length of the shop, still no one politely followed.

Seeing from this that some extraordinary revolution had occurred in the jewelry business I went with my curiosity well aroused to a queer old person half demon and half man who has an idol-shop in a byway of the City and who keeps me informed of affairs of the Edge of the World. And briefly over a pinch of heather incense that he takes by way of snuff he gave me this tremendous information: that Mr. Neepy Thang the son of Thangobrind had returned from the Edge of the World and was even now in London.

The information may not appear tremendous to those unacquainted with the source of jewelry; but when I say that the only thief employed by any West-end jeweller since famous Thangobrind's distressing doom is this same Neepy Thang, and that for lightness of fingers and swiftness of stockinged foot they have none better in Paris, it will be understood why the Bond-street jewellers no longer cared what became of their old stock.

There were big diamonds in London that summer and a few considerable sapphires. In certain astounding kingdoms behind the East strange sovereigns missed from their turbans the heirlooms of ancient wars, and here and there the keepers of crown jewels who had not heard the stockinged feet of Thang, were questioned and died slowly.

And the jewellers gave a little dinner to Thang at the Hotel Great Magnificent; the windows had not been opened for five years and there was wine at a guinea a bottle that you could not tell from champagne and cigars at half a crown with a Havana label. Altogether it was a splendid evening for Thang.

But I have to tell of a far sadder thing than a dinner at a hotel. The public require jewelry and jewelry must be obtained. I have to tell of Neepy Thang's last journey.

That year the fashion was emeralds. A man named Green had recently crossed the Channel on a bicycle and the jewellers said that a green stone would be particularly appropriate to commemorate the event and recommended emeralds.

Now a certain money-lender of Cheapside who had just been made a peer had divided his gains into three equal parts; one for the purchase of the peerage, country-house and park, and the twenty thousand pheasants that are absolutely essential, and one for the upkeep of the position, while the third he banked abroad, partly to cheat the native tax-gatherer and partly because it seemed to him that the days of the Peerage were few and that he might at any moment be called upon to start afresh elsewhere. In the upkeep of the position he included jewellry for his wife and so it came about that Lord Castlenorman placed an order with two well-known Bond-street jewellers named Messrs. Grosvenor and Campbell to the extent of £100,000 for a few reliable emeralds.

But the emeralds in stock were mostly small and shop-soiled and Neepy Thang had to set out at once before he had had as much as a week in London. I will briefly sketch his project. Not many knew it, for where the form of business is blackmail the fewer creditors you have the better (which of course in various degrees applies at all times).

On the shores of the risky seas of Shiroora Shan grows one tree only so that upon its branches if anywhere in the world there must build its nest the Bird of the Difficult Eye. Neepy Thang had come by this information, which was indeed the truth, that if the bird migrated to Fairyland before the three eggs hatched out they would undoubtedly all turn into emeralds, while if they hatched out first it would be a bad business.

When he had mentioned these eggs to

Messrs. Grosvenor and Campbell they had said, "The very thing": they were men of few words, in English, for it was not their native tongue.

So Neepy Thang set out. He bought the purple ticket at Victoria Station. He went by Herne Hill, Bromley and Bickley and passed St. Mary Cray. At Eynsford he changed and taking a footpath along a winding valley went wandering into the hills. And at the top of a hill in a little wood, where all the anemones long since were over and the perfume of mint and thyme from outside came drifting in with Thang, he found once more the familiar path, age-old and fair as wonder, that leads to the Edge of the World. Little to him were its sacred memories that are one with the secret of earth, for he was out on business, and little would they be to me if I ever put them on paper. Let it suffice that he went down that path going further and further from the fields we know, and all the way he muttered to himself, "What if the eggs hatch out and it be a bad business!" The glamour that is at all times upon those lonely lands that lie at the back of the

chalky hills of Kent intensified as he went
upon his journeys. Queerer and queerer
grew the things that he saw by little World-
End Path. Many a twilight descended
upon that journey with all their mysteries,
many a blaze of stars; many a morning came
flaming up to a tinkle of silvern horns; till
the outpost elves of Fairyland came in sight
and the glittering crests of Fairyland's three
mountains betokened the journey's end.
And so with painful steps (for the shores of
the world are covered with huge crystals)
he came to the risky seas of Shiroora Shan
and saw them pounding to gravel the
wreckage of fallen stars, saw them and
heard their roar, those shipless seas that
between earth and the fairies' homes
heave beneath some huge wind that is
none of our four. And there in the darkness on the grizzly coast, for darkness
was swooping slantwise down the sky as
though with some evil purpose, there stood
that lonely, gnarled and deciduous tree.
It was a bad place to be found in after
dark, and night descended with multitudes
of stars, beasts prowling in the blackness
gluttered * at Neepy Thang. And there on

* See any dictionary, but in vain.

58

THERE STOOD THAT LONELY, GNARLED AND DECIDUOUS TREE

a lower branch within easy reach he clearly saw the Bird of the Difficult Eye sitting upon the nest for which she is famous. Her face was towards those three inscrutable mountains, far-off on the other side of the risky seas, whose hidden valleys are Fairyland. Though not yet autumn in the fields we know, it was close on mid-winter here, the moment as Thang knew well when those eggs hatch out. Had he miscalculated and arrived a minute too late? Yet the bird was even now about to migrate, her pinions fluttered and her gaze was toward Fairyland. Thang hoped and muttered a prayer to those pagan gods whose spite and vengeance he had most reason to fear. It seems that it was too late or a prayer too small to placate them, for there and then the stroke of midwinter came and the eggs hatched out in the roar of Shiroora Shan or ever the bird was gone with her difficult eye and it was a bad business indeed for Neepy Thang; I haven't the heart to tell you any more.

"'Ere," said Lord Castlenorman some few weeks later to Messrs. Grosvenor and Campbell, "you aren't 'arf taking your time about those emeralds."

The Long
Porter's Tale

here are things that are known only to the long porter of Tong Tong Tarrup as he sits and mumbles memories to himself in the little bastion gateway.

He remembers the war there was in the halls of the gnomes; and how the fairies came for the opals once, which Tong Tong Tarrup has; and the way that the giants went through the fields below, he watching from his gateway: he remembers quests that are even yet a wonder to the gods. Who dwells in those frozen houses on the high bare brink of the world not even he has told me, and he is held to be garrulous. Among the elves, the only living things ever seen moving at that awful altitude where they quarry turquoise on Earth's highest crag,

his name is a byword for loquacity where-
with they mock the talkative.

His favourite story if you offer him bash
— the drug of which he is fondest, and for
which he will give his service in war to the
elves against the goblins, or vice-versa if the
goblins bring him more — his favourite
story, when bodily soothed by the drug and
mentally fiercely excited, tells of a quest
undertaken ever so long ago for nothing
more marketable than an old woman's song.

Picture him telling it. An old man,
lean and bearded, and almost monstrously
long, that lolled in a city's gateway on a
crag perhaps ten miles high; the houses for
the most part facing eastward, lit by the
sun and moon and the constellations we
know, but one house on the pinnacle looking over the edge of the world and lit by the
glimmer of those unearthly spaces where
one long evening wears away the stars: my
little offering of bash; a long forefinger that
nipped it at once on a stained and greedy
thumb — all these are in the foreground of
the picture. In the background, the mystery of those silent houses and of not knowing who their denizens were, or what service

they had at the hands of the long porter and what payment he had in return, and whether he was mortal.

Picture him in the gateway of this incredible town, having swallowed my bash in silence, stretch his great length, lean back, and begin to speak.

It seems that one clear morning a hundred years ago, a visitor to Tong Tong Tarrup was climbing up from the world. He had already passed above the snow and had set his foot on a step of the earthward stairway that goes down from Tong Tong Tarrup on to the rocks, when the long porter saw him. And so painfully did he climb those easy steps that the grizzled man on watch had long to wonder whether or not the stranger brought him bash, the drug that gives a meaning to the stars and seems to explain the twilight. And in the end there was not a scrap of bash, and the stranger had nothing better to offer that grizzled man than his mere story only.

It seems that the stranger's name was Gerald Jones, and he always lived in London; but once as a child he had been on a Northern moor. It was so long ago that he did not remember how, only somehow or other he walked alone on the moor, and all the ling was in flower. There was nothing in sight but ling and heather and bracken, except, far off near the sunset, on indistinct hills, there were little vague patches that looked like the fields of men. With evening a mist crept up and hid the hills, and still he went walking on over the moor. And then he came to the valley, a tiny valley in the midst of the moor, whose sides were incredibly steep. He lay down and looked at it through the roots of the ling. And a long, long way below him, in a garden by a cottage, with hollyhocks all round her that were taller than herself, there sat an old woman on a wooden chair, singing in the evening. And the man had taken a fancy to the song and remembered it after in London, and whenever it came to his mind it made him think of evenings — the kind you don't get in London — and he heard a soft wind again going idly over the moor and the bumble-bees in a hurry, and forgot the noise of the traffic. And always, whenever he heard men speak of Time, he grudged to Time most this song. Once afterwards he went to that Northern moor again and found the tiny valley, but there was no old woman in the garden, and no one was singing a song. And either regret for the song that the old woman had sung, on a summer evening twenty years away and daily receding, troubled his mind, or else the wearisome work that he did in London, for he worked for a great firm that was perfectly useless; and he grew old early, as men do in cities. And at last, when melancholy brought only regret and the uselessness of his work gained ground with age, he decided to consult a magician. So to a magician he went and told him his troubles, and particularly he told him how he had heard the song. "And now," he said, "it is nowhere in the world."

"Of course it is not in the world," the magician said, "but over the Edge of the World you may easily find it." And he told the man that he was suffering from flux of time and recommended a day at the Edge of the World. Jones asked what part of the Edge of the World he should go to, and the magician had heard Tong Tong Tarrup well spoken of; so he paid him, as is usual,

64

in opals, and started at once on the journey.
The ways to that town are winding; he took
the ticket at Victoria Station that they only
give if they know you: he went past Bleth:
he went along the Hills of Neol-Hungar and
came to the Gap of Poy. All these are in
that part of the world that pertains to the
fields we know; but beyond the Gap of Poy
on those ordinary plains, that so closely
resemble Sussex, one first meets the unlikely.
A line of common grey hills, the Hills of
Sneg, may be seen at the edge of the plain
from the Gap of Poy; it is there that the
incredible begins, infrequently at first, but
happening more and more as you go up the
hills. For instance, descending once into
Poy Plains, the first thing that I saw was an
ordinary shepherd watching a flock of ordinary sheep. I looked at them for some
time and nothing happened, when, without
a word, one of the sheep walked up to the
shepherd and borrowed his pipe and smoked
it — an incident that struck me as unlikely;
but in the Hills of Sneg I met an honest
politician. Over these plains went Jones
and over the Hills of Sneg, meeting at first
unlikely things, and then incredible things,

till he came to the long slope beyond the hills that leads up to the Edge of the World, and where, as all guide-books tell, anything may happen. You might at the foot of this slope see here and there things that could conceivably occur in the fields we know; but soon these disappeared, and the traveller saw nothing but fabulous beasts, browsing on flowers as astounding as themselves, and rocks so distorted that their shapes had clearly a meaning, being too startling to be accidental. Even the trees were shockingly unfamiliar, they had so much to say, and they leant over to one another whenever they spoke and struck grotesque attitudes and leered. Jones saw two fir-trees fighting. The effect of these scenes on his nerves was very severe; still he climbed on, and was much cheered at last by the sight of a primrose, the only familiar thing he had seen for hours, but it whistled and skipped away. He saw the unicorns in their secret valley. Then night in a sinister way slipped over the sky, and there shone not only the stars, but lesser and greater moons, and he heard dragons rattling in the dark.

With dawn there appeared above him among its amazing crags the town of Tong Tong Tarrup, with the light on its frozen stairs, a tiny cluster of houses far up in the sky. He was on the steep mountain now: great mists were leaving it slowly, and revealing, as they trailed away, more and more astonishing things.   Before the mist had all gone he heard quite near him, on what he had thought was bare mountain, the sound of a heavy galloping on turf.   He had come to the plateau of the centaurs.   And all at once he saw them in the mist: there they were, the children of fable, five enormous centaurs. Had he paused on account of any astonishment he had not come so far: he strode on over the plateau, and came quite near to the centaurs.   It is never the centaurs' wont to notice men; they pawed the ground and shouted to one another in Greek, but they said no word to him.   Nevertheless they turned and stared at him when he left them, and when he had crossed the plateau and still went on, all five of them cantered after to the edge of their green land; for above the high green plateau of the centaurs is nothing but naked mountain, and the last green thing that is seen by the mountaineer as he travels to Tong Tong Tarrup is the grass that the centaurs trample. He came into the snow fields that the mountain wears like a cape, its head being bare above it, and still climbed on. The centaurs watched him with increasing wonder.

Not even fabulous beasts were near him now, nor strange demoniac trees — nothing but snow and the clean bare crag above it on which was Tong Tong Tarrup. All day he climbed and evening found him above the snow-line; and soon he came to the stairway cut in the rock and in sight of that grizzled man, the long porter of Tong Tong Tarrup, sitting mumbling amazing memories to himself and expecting in vain from the stranger a gift of bash.

It seems that as soon as the stranger arrived at the bastion gateway, tired though he was, he demanded lodgings at once that commanded a good view of the Edge of the World. But the long porter, that grizzled man, disappointed of his bash, demanded the stranger's story to add to his memories before he would show him the way. And this is the story, if the long porter has told

me the truth and if his memory is still what
it was. And when the story was told, the
grizzled man arose, and, dangling his musi-
cal keys, went up through door after door
and by many stairs and led the stranger to
the top-most house, the highest roof in the
world, and in its parlour showed him the
parlour window. There the tired stranger
sat down in a chair and gazed out of the
window sheer over the Edge of the World.
The window was shut, and in its glittering
panes the twilight of World's Edge blazed
and danced, partly like glow-worms' lamps
and partly like the sea; it went by rippling,
full of wonderful moons. But the traveller
did not look at the wonderful moons. For
from the abyss there grew with their roots
in far constellations a row of hollyhocks,
and amongst them a small green garden
quivered and trembled as scenes tremble in
water; higher up, ling in bloom was floating
upon the twilight, more and more floated
up till all the twilight was purple; the little
green garden low down was hung in the
midst of it. And the garden down below,
and the ling all round it, seemed all to be
trembling and drifting on a song. For the

twilight was full of a song that sang and rang along the edges of the World, and the green garden and the ling seemed to flicker and ripple with it as the song rose and fell, and an old woman was singing it down in the garden. A bumble-bee sailed across from over the Edge of the World. And the song that was lapping there against the coasts of the World, and to which the stars were dancing, was the same that he had heard the old woman sing long since down in the valley in the midst of the Northern moor.

But that grizzled man, the long porter, would not let the stranger stay, because he brought him no bash, and impatiently he shouldered him away, himself not troubling to glance through the World's outermost window, for the lands that Time afflicts and the spaces that Time knows not are all one to that grizzled man, and the bash that he eats more profoundly astounds his mind than anything man can show him either in the World we know or over the Edge. And, bitterly protesting, the traveller went back and down again to the World.

. . . . . .

The Last Book of Wonder

Accustomed as I am to the incredible from knowing the Edge of the World, the story presents difficulties to me. Yet it may be that the devastation wrought by Time is merely local, and that outside the scope of his destruction old songs are still being sung by those that we deem dead. I try to hope so. And yet the more I investigate the story that the long porter told me in the town of Tong Tong Tarrup the more plausible the alternative theory appears — that that grizzled man is a liar.

The Loot of Loma

oming back laden with the loot of Loma, the four tall men looked earnestly to the right; to the left they durst not, for the precipice there that had been with them so long went sickly down on to a bank of clouds, and how much further below that only their fears could say.

Loma lay smoking, a city of ruin, behind them, all its defenders dead; there was no one left to pursue them, and yet their Indian instincts told them that all was scarcely well. They had gone three days along that narrow ledge: mountain quite smooth, incredible, above them, and precipice as smooth and as far below. It was chilly there in the mountains; at night a stream or a wind in the gloom of the chasm

THEY HAD GONE THREE DAYS ALONG THAT NARROW LEDGE

below them went like a whisper; the stillness of all things else began to wear the nerve — an enemy's howl would have braced them; they began to wish their perilous path were wider, they began to wish that they had not sacked Loma.

Had that path been any wider the sacking of Loma must indeed have been harder for them, for the citizens must have fortified the city but that the awful narrowness of that ten-league pass of the hills had made their crag-surrounded city secure. And at last an Indian had said, "Come, let us sack it." Grimly they laughed in the wigwams. Only the eagles, they said, had ever seen it, its hoard of emeralds and its golden gods; and one had said he would reach it, and they answered, "Only the eagles."

It was Laughing Face who said it, and who gathered thirty braves and led them into Loma with their tomahawks and their bows; there were only four left now, but they had the loot of Loma on a mule. They had four golden gods, a hundred emeralds, fifty-two rubies, a large silver gong, two sticks of malachite with amethyst handles for holding incense at religious feasts, four beakers one foot high, each carved from a rose-quartz crystal; a little coffer carved out of two diamonds, and (had they but known it) the written curse of a priest. It was written on parchment in an unknown tongue, and had been slipped in with the loot by a dying hand.

From either end of that narrow, terrible ledge the third night was closing in; it was dropping down on them from the heights of the mountain and slipping up to them out of the abyss, the third night since Loma blazed and they had left it. Three more days of tramping should bring them in triumph home, and yet their instincts said that all was scarcely well. We who sit at home and draw the blinds and shut the shutters as soon as night appears, who gather round the fire when the wind is wild, who pray at regular seasons and in familiar shrines, know little of the demoniac look of night when it is filled with curses of false, infuriated gods. Such a night was this. Though in the heights the fleecy clouds were idle, yet the wind was stirring mournfully in the abyss and moaning as it stirred, unhappily at first and full of sorrow; but as day turned away from that awful path a very definite menace entered its voice which fast grew louder and louder, and night came on with a long howl. Shadows repeatedly passed over the stars, and then a mist fell swiftly, as though there were something suddenly to be done and utterly to be hidden, as in very truth there was.

And in the chill of that mist the four tall men prayed to their totems, the whimsical wooden figures that stood so far away, watching the pleasant wigwams; the fire-light even now would be dancing over their faces, while there would come to their ears delectable tales of war. They halted upon the pass and prayed, and waited for any sign. For a man's totem may be in the likeness perhaps of an otter, and a man may pray, and if his totem be placable and watching over his man a noise may be heard at once like the noise that the otter makes, though it be but a stone that falls on another stone; and the noise is a sign. The four men's totems that stood so far away were in the likeness of the coney, the bear, the heron, and the lizard. They waited, and no sign came. With all the noises of the wind in the abyss, no noise was like the thump that the coney makes, nor the bear's growl, nor the heron's screech, nor the rustle of the lizard in the reeds.

It seemed that the wind was saying something over and over again, and that that thing was evil. They prayed again to their totems, and no sign came. And then they knew that there was some power that night that was prevailing against the pleasant carvings on painted poles of wood with the firelight on their faces so far away. Now it was clear that the wind was saying something, some very, very dreadful thing in a tongue that they did not know. They listened, but they could not tell what it said. Nobody could have said from seeing their faces how much the four tall men desired the wigwams again, desired the camp-fire and the tales of war and the benignant totems that listened and smiled in the dusk: Nobody could have seen how well they knew that this was no common night or wholesome mist.

When at last no answer came nor any sign from their totems, they pulled out of the bag those golden gods that Loma gave not up except in flames and when all her men were dead. They had large ruby eyes and emerald tongues. They set them down upon that mountain pass, the cross-legged idols with their emerald tongues; and having placed between them a few decent yards, as it seemed meet there should be between gods and men, they bowed them down and prayed in their desperate straits in that dank, ominous night to the gods they had wronged, for it seemed that there was a vengeance upon the hills and that they would scarce escape, as the wind knew well. And the gods laughed, all four, and wagged their emerald tongues; the Indians saw them, though the night had fallen and though the mist was low. The four tall men leaped up at once from their knees and would have left the gods upon the pass but that they feared some hunter of their tribe might one day find them and say of Laughing Face, "He fled and left behind his golden gods," and sell the gold and come with his wealth to the wigwams and be greater than Laughing Face and his three men. And then they would have cast the gods away, down the abyss, with their eyes and their emerald tongues, but they knew that enough already they had wronged Loma's gods, and feared that vengeance enough was waiting them on the hills. So they packed them back in the bag on the frightened mule, the bag that held the curse they knew nothing of, and so pushed on into the menacing night. Till midnight they plodded on and would not sleep; grimmer and grimmer grew the look of the night, and the wind more full of meaning, and the mule knew and trembled, and it seemed that the wind knew, too, as did the instincts of those four tall men, though they could not reason it out, try how they would.

And though the squaws waited long where the pass winds out of the mountains, near where the wigwams are upon the plains, the wigwams and the totems and the fire, and though they watched by day, and for many nights uttered familiar calls, still did they never see those four tall men emerge out of the mountains any more, even though they prayed to their totems upon their painted poles; but the curse in the mystical writing that they had unknown in their bag worked there on that lonely pass six leagues from the ruins of Loma, and nobody can tell us what it was.

The Secret of the Sea

I n an ill-lit ancient tavern that I know, are many tales of the sea; but not without the wine of Gorgondy, that I had of a private bargain from the gnomes, was the tale laid bare for which I had waited of an evening for the greater part of a year.

I knew my man and listened to his stories, sitting amid the bluster of his oaths; I plied him with rum and whiskey and mixed drinks, but there never came the tale for which I sought, and as a last resort I went to the Huthneth Mountains and bargained there all night with the chiefs of the gnomes.

When I came to the ancient tavern and entered the low-roofed room, bringing the hoard of the gnomes in a bottle of hammered iron, my man had not yet arrived. The sailors laughed at my old iron bottle, but I sat down and waited; had I opened it then they would have wept and sung. I was well content to wait, for I knew my man had the story, and it was such a one as had profoundly stirred the incredulity of the faithless.

He entered and greeted me, and sat down and called for brandy. He was a hard man to turn from his purpose, and, uncorking my iron bottle, I sought to dissuade him from brandy for fear that when the brandy, bit his throat he should refuse to leave it for any other wine. He lifted his head and said deep and dreadful things of any man that should dare to speak against brandy,

I swore that I said nothing against brandy but added that it was often given to children, while Gorgondy was only drunk by men of such depravity that they had abandoned sin because all the usual vices had come to seem genteel. When he asked if Gorgondy was a bad wine to drink I said that it was so bad that if a man sipped it that was the one touch that made damnation certain. Then he asked me what I had in the iron bottle, and I said it was

Gorgondy; and then he shouted for the largest tumbler in that ill-lit ancient tavern, and stood up and shook his fist at me when it came, and swore, and told me to fill it with the wine that I got on that bitter night from the treasure house of the gnomes.

As he drank it he told me that he had met men who had spoken against wine, and that they had mentioned Heaven; and therefore he would not go there — no, not he; and that once he had sent one of them to Hell, but when he got there he would turn him out, and he had no use for milksops.

Over the second tumbler he was thoughtful, but still he said no word of the tale he knew, until I feared that it would never be heard. But when the third glass of that terrific wine had burned its way down his gullet, and vindicated the wickedness of the gnomes, his reticence withered like a leaf in the fire, and he bellowed out the secret.

I had long known that there is in ships a will or way of their own, and had even suspected that when sailors die or abandon their ships at sea, a derelict, being left to her own devices, may seek her own ends;

but I had never dreamed by night, or fancied during the day, that the ships had a god that they worshipped, or that they secretly slipped away to a temple in the sea.

Over the fourth glass of the wine that the gnomes so sinfully brew but have kept so wisely from man, until the bargain that I had with their elders all through that autumn night, the sailor told me the story. I do not tell it as he told it to me because of the oaths that were in it; nor is it from delicacy that I refrain from writing these oaths verbatim, but merely because the horror they caused in me at the time troubles me still whenever I put them on paper, and I continue to shudder until I have blotted them out. Therefore, I tell the story in my own words, which, if they possess a certain decency that was not in the mouth of that sailor, unfortunately do not smack, as his did, of rum and blood and the sea.

You would take a ship to be a dead thing like a table, as dead as bits of iron and canvas and wood. That is because you always live on shore, and have never seen the sea, and drink milk. Milk is a more accursed drink than water.

What with the captain and what with the man at the wheel, and what with the crew, a ship has no fair chance of showing a will of her own.

There is only one moment in the history of ships, that carry crews on board, when they act by their own free will. This moment comes when all the crew are drunk. As the last man falls drunk on to the deck, the ship is free of man, and immediately slips away. She slips away at once on a new course and is never one yard out in a hundred miles.

It was like this one night with the Sea-Fancy. Bill Smiles was there himself, and can vouch for it. Bill Smiles has never told this tale before for fear that anyone should call him a liar. Nobody dislikes being hung as much as Bill Smiles would, but he won't be called a liar. I tell the tale as I heard it, relevancies and irrelevancies, though in my more decent words; and as I made no doubts of the truth of it then, I hardly like to now; others can please themselves.

It is not often that the whole of a crew is drunk. The crew of the Sea-Fancy was no drunkener than others. It happened like this.

The captain was always drunk. One day a fancy he had that some spiders were plotting against him, or a sudden bleeding he had from both his ears, made him think that drinking might be bad for his health. Next day he signed the pledge. He was sober all that morning and all the afternoon, but at evening he saw a sailor drinking a a glass of beer, and a fit of madness seized him, and he said things that seemed bad to Bill Smiles. And next morning he made all of them take the pledge.

For two days nobody had a drop to drink, unless you count water, and on the third morning the captain was quite drunk It stood to reason they all had a glass or two then, except the man at the wheel; and towards evening the man at the wheel could bear it no longer, and seems to have had his glass like all the rest, for the ship's course wobbled a bit and made a circle or two. Then all of a sudden she went off south by east under full canvas till midnight, and never altered her course. And at midnight she came to the wide wet courts of the Temple in the Sea.

People who think that Mr. Smiles is drunk often make a great mistake. And people are not the only ones that have made that mistake. Once a ship made it, and a lot of ships. It's a mistake to think that old Bill Smiles is drunk just because he can't move.

Midnight and moonlight and the Temple in the Sea Bill Smiles clearly remembers, and all the derelicts in the world were there, the old abandoned ships. The figureheads were nodding to themselves and blinking at the image. The image was a woman of white marble on a pedestal in the outer court of the Temple of the Sea: she was clearly the love of all the man-deserted ships, or the goddess to whom they prayed their heathen prayers. And as Bill Smiles was watching them, the lips of the figureheads moved; they all began to pray. But all at once their lips were closed with a snap when they saw that there were men on the Sea-Fancy. They all came crowding up and nodded and nodded and nodded to see if all were drunk, and that's when they made their mistake about old Bill Smiles, although he couldn't move. They would

MIDNIGHT AND MOONLIGHT AND THE TEMPLE IN THE SEA

have given up the treasuries of the gulfs sooner than let men hear the prayers they said or guess their love for the goddess. It is the intimate secret of the sea.

The sailor paused. And, in my eagerness to hear what lyrical or blasphemous thing those figureheads prayed by moonlight at midnight in the sea to the woman of marble who was a goddess to ships, I pressed on the sailor more of my Gorgondy wine that the gnomes so wickedly brew.

I should never have done it; but there he was sitting silent while the secret was almost mine. He took it moodily and drank a glass; and with the other glasses that he had had he fell a prey to the villainy of the gnomes who brew this unbridled wine to no good end. His body leaned forward slowly, then fell on to the table, his face being sideways and full of a wicked smile, and, saying very clearly the one word, "Hell," he became silent for ever with the secret he had from the sea.

How Ali Came
to the Black Country

Shooshan the barber went to Shep the maker of teeth to discuss the state of England. They agreed that it was time to send for Ali.

So Shooshan stepped late that night from the little shop near Fleet Street and made his way back again to his house in the ends of London and sent at once the message that brought Ali.

And Ali came, mostly on foot, from the country of Persia, and it took him a year to come; but when he came he was welcome.

And Shep told Ali what was the matter with England and Shooshan swore that it was so, and Ali looking out of the window of the little shop near Fleet Street beheld the ways of London and audibly blessed King Solomon and his seal.

When Shep and Shooshan heard the
names of King Solomon and his seal both
asked, as they had scarcely dared before,
if Ali had it. Ali patted a little bundle of
silks that he drew from his inner raiment.
It was there.

Now concerning the movements and
courses of the stars and the influence on
them of spirits of Earth and devils this age
has been rightly named by some The Second
Age of Ignorance. But Ali knew. And
by watching nightly, for seven nights in
Bagdad, the way of certain stars he had
found out the dwelling place of Him they
Needed.

Guided by Ali all three set forth for the
Midlands. And by the reverence that was
manifest in the faces of Shep and Shooshan
towards the person of Ali, some knew what
Ali carried, while others said that it was the
tablets of the Law, others the name of God,
and others that he must have a lot of money
about him. So they passed Slod and
Apton.

And at last they came to the town for
which Ali sought, that spot over which he
had seen the shy stars wheel and swerve

away from their orbits, being troubled. Verily when they came there were no stars, though it was midnight. And Ali said that it was the appointed place. In harems in Persia in the evening when the tales go round it is still told how Ali and Shep and Shooshan came to the Black country.

When it was dawn they looked upon the country and saw how it was without doubt the appointed place, even as Ali had said, for the earth had been taken out of pits and burned and left lying in heaps, and there were many factories, and they stood over the town and as it were rejoiced. And with one voice Shep and Shooshan gave praise to Ali.

And Ali said that the great ones of the place must needs be gathered together, and to this end Shep and Shooshan went into the town and there spoke craftily. For they said that Ali had of his wisdom contrived as it were a patent and a novelty which should greatly benefit England. And when they heard how he sought nothing for his novelty save only to benefit mankind they consented to speak with Ali and see his novelty. And they came forth and met Ali.

GUIDED BY ALI, ALL THREE SET FORTH FOR THE MIDLANDS

And Ali spake and said unto them: "O lords of this place; in the book that all men know it is written how that a fisherman casting his net into the sea drew up a bottle of brass, and when he took the stopper from the bottle a dreadful genie of horrible aspect rose from the bottle, as it were like a smoke, even to darkening the sky, whereat the fisherman . . ." And the great ones of that place said: "We have heard the story." And Ali said: "What became of that genie after he was safely thrown back into the sea is not properly spoken of by any save those that pursue the study of demons and not with certainty by any man, but that the stopper that bore the ineffable seal and bears it to this day became separate from the bottle is among those things that man may know." And when there was doubt among the great ones Ali drew forth his bundle and one by one removed those many silks till the seal stood revealed; and some of them knew it for the seal and others knew it not.

And they looked curiously at it and listened to Ali, and Ali said:

"Having heard how evil is the case of

England, how a smoke has darkened the country, and in places (as men say) the grass is black, and how even yet your factories multiply, and haste and noise have become such that men have no time for song, I have therefore come at the bidding of my good friend Shooshan, barber of London, and of Shep, a maker of teeth, to make things well with you."

And they said: "But where is your patent and your novelty?"

And Ali said: "Have I not here the stopper and on it, as good men know, the ineffable seal? Now I have learned in Persia how that your trains that make the haste, and hurry men to and fro, and your factories and the digging of your pits and all the things that are evil are every one of them caused and brought about by steam."

"Is it not so?" said Shooshan.

"It is even so," said Shep.

"Now it is clear," said Ali, "that the chief devil that vexes England and has done all this harm, who herds men into cities and will not let them rest, is even the devil Steam."

Then the great ones would have rebuked

him but one said: "No, let us hear him, perhaps his patent may improve on steam."

And to them hearkening Ali went on thus: "O Lords of this place, let there be made a bottle of strong steel, for I have no bottle with my stopper, and this being done let all the factories, trains, digging of pits, and all evil things soever that may be done by steam be stopped for seven days, and the men that tend them shall go free, but the steel bottle for my stopper I will leave open in a likely place. Now that chief devil, Steam, finding no factories to enter into, nor no trains, sirens nor pits prepared for him, and being curious and accustomed to steel pots, will verily enter one night into the bottle that you shall make for my stopper, and I shall spring forth from my hiding with my stopper and fasten him down with the ineffable seal which is the seal of King Solomon and deliver him up to you that you cast him into the sea."

And the great ones answered Ali and they said: "But what should we gain if we lose our prosperity and be no longer rich?"

And Ali said: "When we have cast this devil into the sea there will come back again the woods and ferns and all the beautiful things that the world hath, the little leaping hares shall be seen at play, there shall be music on the hills again, and at twilight ease and quiet and after the twilight stars."

And "Verily," said Shooshan, "there shall be the dance again."

"Aye," said Shep, "there shall be the country dance."

But the great ones spake and said, denying Ali: "We will make no such bottle for your stopper nor stop our healthy factories or good trains, nor cease from our digging of pits nor do anything that you desire, for an interference with steam would strike at the roots of that prosperity that you see so plentifully all around us."

Thus they dismissed Ali there and then from that place where the earth was torn up and burnt, being taken out of pits, and where factories blazed all night with a demoniac glare; and they dismissed with him both Shooshan, the barber, and Shep, the maker of teeth: so that a week later Ali started from Calais on his long walk back to Persia.

The Last Book of Wonder

And all this happened thirty years ago, and Shep is an old man now and Shooshan older, and many mouths have bit with the teeth of Shep (for he has a knack of getting them back whenever his customers die), and they have written again to Ali away in the country of Persia with these words, saying:

"O Ali. The devil has indeed begotten a devil, even that spirit Petrol. And the young devil waxeth, and increaseth in lustihood and is ten years old and becoming like to his father. Come therefore and help us with the ineffable seal. For there is none like Ali."

And Ali turns where his slaves scatter rose-leaves, letting the letter fall, and deeply draws from his hookah a puff of the scented smoke, right down into his lungs, and sighs it forth and smiles, and lolling round on to his other elbow speaks comfortably and says, "And shall a man go twice to the help of a dog?"

And with these words he thinks no more of England but ponders again the inscrutable ways of God.

The Bureau D'Echange De Maux

I often think of the Bureau d'Echange de Maux and the wondrously evil old man that sate therein. It stood in a little street that there is in Paris, its doorway made of three brown beams of wood, the top one overlapping the others like the Greek letter *pi*, all the rest painted green, a house far lower and narrower than its neighbours and infinitely stranger, a thing to take one's fancy. And over the doorway on the old brown beam in faded yellow letters this legend ran, Bureau Universel d'Echanges de Maux.

I entered at once and accosted the listless man that lolled on a stool by his counter. I demanded the wherefore of his wonderful house, what evil wares he exchanged, with many other things that I wished to know, for curiosity led me; and indeed had it not I had gone at once from the shop, for there was so evil a look in that fattened man, in the hang of his fallen cheeks and his sinful eye, that you would have said he had had dealings with Hell and won the advantage by sheer wickedness.

Such a man was mine host; but above all the evil of him lay in his eyes, which lay so still, so apathetic, that you would have sworn that he was drugged or dead; like lizards motionless on a wall they lay, then suddenly they darted, and all his cunning flamed up and revealed itself in what one moment before seemed no more than a sleepy and ordinary wicked old man. And this was the object and trade of that peculiar shop, the Bureau Universel d'E-changes de Maux: you paid twenty francs, which the old man proceeded to take from me, for admission to the bureau and then had the right to exchange any evil or mis-fortune with anyone on the premises for some evil or misfortune that he "could afford," as the old man put it.

There were four or five men in the dingy

ends of that low-ceilinged room who gesticulated and muttered softly in twos as men who make a bargain, and now and then more came in, and the eyes of the flabby owner of the house leaped up at them as they entered, seemed to know their errands at once and each one's peculiar need, and fell back again into somnolence, receiving his twenty francs in an almost lifeless hand and biting the coin as though in pure absence of mind.

"Some of my clients," he told me. So amazing to me was the trade of this extraordinary shop that I engaged the old man in conversation, repulsive though he was, and from his garrulity I gathered these facts. He spoke in perfect English though his utterance was somewhat thick and heavy; no language seemed to come amiss to him. He had been in business a great many years, how many he would not say, and was far older than he looked. All kinds of people did business in his shop. What they exchanged with each other he did not care except that it had to be evils, he was not empowered to carry on any other kind of business.

There was no evil, he told me, that was not negotiable there; no evil the old man knew had ever been taken away in despair from his shop. A man might have to wait and come back again next day, and next day and the day after, paying twenty francs each time, but the old man had the addresses of his clients and shrewdly knew their needs, and soon the right two met and eagerly changed their commodities. "Commodities" was the old man's terrible word, said with a gruesome smack of his heavy lips, for he took a pride in his business and evils to him were goods.

I learned from him in ten minutes very much of human nature, more than I have ever learned from any other man; I learned from him that a man's own evil is to him the worst thing that there is or could be, and that an evil so unbalances all men's minds that they always seek for extremes in that small grim shop. A woman that had no children had exchanged with an impoverished half-maddened creature with twelve. On one occasion a man had exchanged wisdom for folly.

"Why on earth did he do that?" I said.

"None of my business," the old man answered in his heavy indolent way. He merely took his twenty francs from each and ratified the agreement in the little room at the back opening out of the shop where his clients do business. Apparently the man that had parted with wisdom had left the shop upon the tips of his toes with a happy though foolish expression all over his face, but the other went thoughtfully away wearing a troubled and very puzzled look. Almost always it seemed they did business in opposite evils.

But the thing that puzzled me most in all my talks with that unwieldy man, the thing that puzzles me still, is that none that had once done business in that shop ever returned again; a man might come day after day for many weeks, but once do business and he never returned; so much the old man told me, but when I asked him why, he only muttered that he did not know.

It was to discover the wherefore of this strange thing and for no other reason at all that I determined myself to do business sooner or later in the little room at the back of that mysterious shop. I determined to exchange some very trivial evil for some evil equally slight, to seek for myself an advantage so very small as scarcely to give Fate as it were a grip, for I deeply distrusted these bargains, knowing well that man has never yet benefited by the marvellous and that the more miraculous his advantage appears to be the more securely and tightly do the gods or the witches catch him. In a few days more I was going back to England and I was beginning to fear that I should be sea-sick: this fear of sea-sickness, not the actual malady but only the mere fear of it, I decided to exchange for a suitably little evil. I did not know with whom I should be dealing, who in reality was the head of the firm (one never does when shopping) but I decided that neither Jew nor Devil could make very much on so small a bargain as that.

I told the old man my project, and he scoffed at the smallness of my commodity trying to urge me to some darker bargain, but could not move me from my purpose. And then he told me tales with a somewhat boastful air of the big business, the great bargains that had passed through his hands.

A man had once run in there to try and exchange death, he had swallowed poison by accident and had only twelve hours to live. That sinister old man had been able to oblige him. A client was willing to exchange the commodity.

"But what did he give in exchange for death?" I said.

"Life," said that grim old man with a furtive chuckle.

"It must have been a horrible life," I said.

"That was not my affair," the proprietor said, lazily rattling together as he spoke a little pocketful of twenty-franc pieces.

Strange business I watched in that shop for the next few days, the exchange of odd commodities, and heard strange mutterings in corners amongst couples who presently rose and went to the back room, the old man following to ratify.

Twice a day for a week I paid my twenty francs, watching life with its great needs and its little needs morning and afternoon spread out before me in all its wonderful variety.

And one day I met a comfortable man

with only a little need, he seemed to have the very evil I wanted. He always feared the lift was going to break. I knew too much of hydraulics to fear things as silly as that, but it was not my business to cure his ridiculous fear. Very few words were needed to convince him that mine was the evil for him, he never crossed the sea, and I on the other hand could always walk upstairs, and I also felt at the time, as many must feel in that shop, that so absurd a fear could never trouble me. And yet at times it is almost the curse of my life. When we both had signed the parchment in the spidery back room and the old man had signed and ratified (for which we had to pay him fifty francs each) I went back to my hotel, and there I saw the deadly thing in the basement. They asked me if I would go upstairs in the lift, from force of habit I risked it, and I held my breath all the way and clenched my hands. Nothing will induce me to try such a journey again. I would sooner go up to my room in a balloon. And why? Because if a balloon goes wrong you have a chance, it may spread out into a parachute after it has burst, it may catch in a tree, a hundred

103

and one things may happen, but if the lift falls down its shaft you are done. As for sea-sickness I shall never be sick again, I cannot tell you why except that I know that it is so.

And the shop in which I made this remarkable, bargain the shop to which none return when their business is done: I set out for it next day. Blindfold I could have found my way to the unfashionable quarter out of which a mean street runs, where you take the alley at the end, whence runs the cul de sac where the queer shop stood. A shop with pillars, fluted and painted red, stands on its near side, its other neighbour is a low-class jeweller's with little silver brooches in the window. In such incongruous company stood the shop with beams with its walls painted green.

In half an hour I stood in the cul de sac to which I had gone twice a day for the last week, I found the shop with the ugly painted pillars and the jeweller that sold brooches, but the green house with the three beams was gone.

Pulled down, you will say, although in a single night. That can never be the answer to the mystery, for the house of the fluted pillars painted on plaster and the low-class jeweller's shop with its silver brooches (all of which I could identify one by one) were standing side by side.

A Story of Land and Sea

It is written in the first Book
of Wonder how Captain Shard
of the bad ship Desperate
Lark, having looted the sea-
coast city Bombasharna, retired from active life; and
resigning piracy to younger men, with the
good will of the North and South Atlantic,
settled down with a captured queen on his
floating island.

Sometimes he sank a ship for the sake of
old times but he no longer hovered along the
trade-routes; and timid merchants watched
for other men.

It was not age that caused him to leave
his romantic profession; nor unworthiness
of its traditions, nor gun-shot wound, nor
drink; but grim necessity and force majeure.

Five navies were after him. How he gave them the slip one day in the Mediterranean, how he fought with the Arabs, how a ship's broadside was heard in Lat. 23 N. Long. 4 E. for the first time and the last, with other things unknown to Admiralties, I shall proceed to tell.

He had had his fling, had Shard, captain of pirates, and all his merry men wore pearls in their ear-rings; and now the English fleet was after him under full sail along the coast of Spain with a good North wind behind them. They were not gaining much on Shard's rakish craft, the bad ship Desperate Lark, yet they were closer than was to his liking, and they interfered with business.

For a day and a night they had chased him, when off Cape St. Vincent at about six a. m. Shard took that step that decided his retirement from active life, he turned for the Mediterranean. Had he held on Southwards down the African coast it is doubtful whether in face of the interference of England, Russia, France, Denmark and Spain, he could have made piracy pay; but in turning for the Mediterranean he took

what we may call the penultimate step of
his life which meant for him settling down.
There were three great courses of action
invented by Shard in his youth, upon which
he pondered by day and brooded by night,
consolations in all his dangers, secret even
from his men, three means of escape as he
hoped from any peril that might meet him
on the sea. One of these was the floating
island that the Book of Wonder tells of,
another was so fantastic that we may doubt
if even the brilliant audacity of Shard could
ever have found it practicable, at least he
never tried it so far as is known in that tavern by the sea in which I glean my news,
and the third he determined on carrying
out as he turned that morning for the Mediterranean. True he might yet have practised piracy in spite of the step that he took,
a little later when the seas grew quiet, but
that penultimate step was like that small
house in the country that the business man
has his eye on, like some snug investment
put away for old age, there are certain final
courses in men's lives which after taking
they never go back to business.

He turned then for the Mediterranean

with the English fleet behind him, and his men wondered.

What madness was this, — muttered Bill the Boatswain in Old Frank's only ear,— with the French fleet waiting in the Gulf of Lyons and the Spaniards all the way between Sardinia and Tunis: for they knew the Spaniards' ways And they made a deputation and waited upon Captain Shard, all of them sober and wearing their costly clothes, and they said that the Mediterranean was a trap, and all he said was that the North wind should hold. And the crew said they were done.

So they entered the Mediterranean and the English fleet came up and closed the straits. And Shard went tacking along the Moroccan coast with a dozen frigates behind him. And the North wind grew in strength. And not till evening did he speak to his crew, and then he gathered them all together except the man at the helm, and politely asked them to come down to the hold. And there he showed them six immense steel axles and a dozen low iron wheels of enormous width which none had seen before; and he told his crew how all unknown to the world his keel had been specially fitted for these same axles and wheels, and how he meant soon to sail to the wide Atlantic again, though not by the way of the straits. And when they heard the name of the Atlantic all his merry men cheered, for they looked on the Atlantic as a wide safe sea.

And night came down and Captain Shard sent for his diver. With the sea getting up it was hard work for the diver, but by midnight things were done to Shard's satisfaction, and the diver said that of all the jobs he had done — but finding no apt comparison, and being in need of a drink, silence fell on him and soon sleep, and his comrades carried him away to his hammock. All the next day the chase went on with the English well in sight, for Shard had lost time overnight with his wheels and axles, and the danger of meeting the Spaniards increased every hour; and evening came when every minute seemed dangerous, yet they still went tacking on towards the East where they knew the Spaniards must be.

And at last they sighted their topsails right ahead, and still Shard went on. It was a close thing, but night was coming on, and the Union Jack which he hoisted helped Shard with the Spaniards for the last few anxious minutes, though it seemed to anger the English, but as Shard said, "There's no pleasing everyone," and then the twilight shivered into darkness.

"Hard to starboard," said Captain Shard.

The North wind which had risen all day was now blowing a gale. I do not know what part of the coast Shard steered for, but Shard knew, for the coasts of the world were to him what Margate is to some of us.

At a place where the desert rolling up from mystery and from death, yea, from the heart of Africa, emerges upon the sea, no less grand than her, no less terrible, even there they sighted the land quite close, almost in darkness. Shard ordered every man to the hinder part of the ship and all the ballast too; and soon the Desperate Lark, her prow a little high out of the water, doing her eighteen knots before the wind, struck a sandy beach and shuddered, she heeled over a little, then righted herself, and slowly headed into the interior of Africa.

The men would have given three cheers, but after the first Shard silenced them and, steering the ship himself, he made them a short speech while the broad wheels pounded slowly over the African sand, doing barely five knots in a gale. The perils of the sea he said had been greatly exaggerated. Ships had been sailing the sea for hundreds of years and at sea you knew what to do, but on land this was different. They were on land now and they were not to forget it. At sea you might make as much noise as you pleased and no harm was done, but on land anything might happen. One of the perils of the land that he instanced was that of hanging. For every hundred men that they hung on land, he said, not more than twenty would be hung at sea. The men were to sleep at their guns. They would not go far that night; for the risk of being wrecked at night was another danger peculiar to the land, while at sea you might sail from set of sun till dawn: yet it was essential to get out of sight of the sea for if anyone knew they were there they'd have cavalry after them. And he had sent back Smerdrak (a young lieutenant of pirates) to cover their tracks where they came up from the sea. And the merry men vigorously nodded their heads though they did not dare to cheer, and presently Smerdrak came running up and they threw him a rope by the stern. And when they had done fifteen knots they anchored, and Captain Shard gathered his men about him and, standing by the land-wheel in the bows, under the large and clear Algerian stars, he explained his system of steering. There was not much to be said for it, he had with considerable ingenuity detached and pivoted the portion of the keel that held the leading axle and could move it by chains which were controlled from the land-wheel, thus the front pair of wheels could be deflected at will, but only very slightly, and they afterwards found that in a hundred yards they could only turn their ship four yards from her course. But let not captains of comfortable battleships, or owners even of yachts, criticise too harshly a man who was not of their time and who knew not modern contrivances; it should be remembered also that Shard was no longer at sea. His steering may have been clumsy but he did what he could.

When the use and limitations of his land-wheel had been made clear to his men, Shard bade them all turn in except those on watch. Long before dawn he woke them and by the very first gleam of light they got their ship under way, so that when those two fleets that had made so sure of Shard closed in like a great crescent on the Algerian coast there was no sign to see of the Desperate Lark either on sea or land; and the flags of the Admiral's ship broke out into a hearty English oath.

The gale blew for three days and, Shard using more sail by daylight, they scudded over the sands at little less than ten knots, though on the report of rough water ahead (as the lookout man called rocks, low hills or uneven surface before he adapted himself to his new surroundings) the rate was much decreased. Those were long summer days and Shard who was anxious while the wind held good to outpace the rumour of his own appearance sailed for nineteen hours a day, lying to at ten in the evening and hoisting sail again at three a. m. when it first began to be light.

In those three days he did five hundred miles; then the wind dropped to a breeze though it still blew from the North, and for a week they did no more than two knots an hour. The merry men began to murmur then. Luck had distinctly favoured Shard at first for it sent him at ten knots through the only populous districts well ahead of crowds except those who chose to run, and the cavalry were away on a local raid. As for the runners they soon dropped off when Shard pointed his cannon though he did not dare to fire, up there near the coast; for much as he jeered at the intelligence of the English and Spanish Admirals in not suspecting his manoeuvre, the only one as he said that was possible in the circumstances, yet he knew that cannon had an obvious sound which would give his secret away to the weakest mind. Certainly luck had befriended him, and when it did so no longer he made out of the occasion all that could be made; for instance while the wind held good he had never missed opportunities to revictual, if he

passed by a village its pigs and poultry
were his, and whenever he passed by water
he filled his tanks to the brim, and now that
he could only do two knots he sailed all
night with a man and a lantern before him:
thus in that week he did close on four
hundred miles while another man would
have anchored at night and have missed five
or six hours out of the twenty-four. Yet
his men murmured. Did he think the wind
would last for ever, they said. And Shard
only smoked. It was clear that he was thinking, and thinking hard. "But what is he
thinking about?" said Bill to Bad Jack.
And Bad Jack answered: "He may think
as hard as he likes but thinking won't get us
out of the Sahara if this wind were to drop."

And towards the end of that week Shard
went to his chart-room and laid a new course
for his ship a little to the East and towards
cultivation. And one day towards evening
they sighted a village, and twilight came
and the wind dropped altogether. Then
the murmurs of the merry men grew to oaths
and nearly to mutiny. "Where were
they now?" they asked, and were they
being treated like poor honest men ?

Shard quieted them by asking what they wished to do themselves and when no one had any better plan than going to the villagers and saying that they had been blown out of their course by a storm, Shard unfolded his scheme to them.

Long ago he had heard how they drove carts with oxen in Africa, oxen were very numerous in these parts wherever there was any cultivation, and for this reason when the wind had begun to drop he had laid his course for the village: that night the moment it was dark they were to drive off fifty yoke of oxen; by midnight they must all be yoked to the bows and then away they would go at a good round gallop.

So fine a plan as this astonished the men and they all apologised for their want of faith in Shard, shaking hands with him every one and spitting on their hands before they did so in token of good will.

The raid that night succeeded admirably, but ingenious as Shard was on land, and a past-master at sea, yet it must be admitted that lack of experience in this class of seamanship led him to make a mistake, a slight one it is true, and one that a little practice would have prevented altogether: the oxen could not gallop. Shard swore at them, threatened them with his pistol, said they should have no food, and all to no avail: that night and as long as they pulled the bad ship Desperate Lark they did one knot an hour and no more. Shard's failures like everything that came his way were used as stones in the edifice of his future success, he went at once to his chart-room and worked out all his calculations anew.

The matter of the oxen's pace made pursuit impossible to avoid. Shard therefore countermanded his order to his lieutenant to cover the tracks in the sand, and the Desperate Lark plodded on into the Sahara on her new course trusting to her guns.

The village was not a large one and the little crowd that was sighted astern next morning disappeared after the first shot from the cannon in the stern. At first Shard made the oxen wear rough iron bits, another of his mistakes, and strong bits too. "For if they run away," he had said, "we might as well be driving before a gale and there's no saying where we'd find ourselves," but after a day or two he found that the bits were no good and, like the practical man he was, immediately corrected his mistake.

And now the crew sang merry songs all day bringing out mandolins and clarionets and cheering Captain Shard. All were jolly except the captain himself whose face was moody and perplexed; he alone expected to hear more of those villagers; and the oxen were drinking up the water every day, he alone feared that there was no more to be had, and a very unpleasant fear that is when your ship is becalmed in a desert. For over a week they went on like this doing ten knots a day and the music and singing got on the captain's nerves, but he dared not tell his men what the trouble was. And then one day the oxen drank up the last of the water. And Lieutenant Smerdrak came and reported the fact.

"Give them rum," said Shard, and he cursed the oxen. "What is good enough for me," he said, "should be good enough for them," and he swore that they should have rum.

"Aye, aye, sir," said the young lieutenant of pirates.

Shard should not be judged by the orders

he gave that day, for nearly a fortnight he had watched the doom that was coming slowly towards him, discipline cut him off from anyone that might have shared his fear and discussed it, and all the while he had had to navigate his ship, which even at sea is an arduous responsibility. These things had fretted the calm of that clear judgment that had once baffled five navies. Therefore he cursed the oxen and ordered them rum, and Smerdrak had said "Aye, aye, sir," and gone below.

Towards sunset Shard was standing on the poop, thinking of death; it would not come to him by thirst; mutiny first, he thought. The oxen were refusing rum for the last time, and the men were beginning to eye Captain Shard in a very ominous way, not muttering, but each man looking at him with a sidelong look of the eye as though there were only one thought among them all that had no need of words. A score of geese like a long letter "V" were crossing the evening sky, they slanted their necks and all went twisting downwards somewhere about the horizon. Captain Shard rushed to his chart-room, and pres-

ently the men came in at the door with Old
Frank in front looking awkward and twisting his cap in his hand.

"What is it?" said Shard as though nothing were wrong.

Then Old Frank said what he had come
to say: "We want to know what you be
going to do."

And the men nodded grimly.

"Get water for the oxen," said Captain
Shard, "as the swine won't have rum, and
they'll have to work for it, the lazy beasts.
Up anchor!"

And at the word water a look came into
their faces like when some wanderer suddenly
thinks of home.

"Water!" they said.

"Why not?" said Captain Shard. And
none of them ever knew that but for those
geese, that slanted their necks and suddenly
twisted downwards, they would have found
no water that night nor ever after, and the
Sahara would have taken them as she has
taken so many and shall take so many more.
All that night they followed their new
course: at dawn they found an oasis and
the oxen drank.

And here, on this green acre or so with its palm-trees and its well, beleaguered by thousands of miles of desert and holding out through the ages, here they decided to stay: for those who have been without water for a while in one of Africa's deserts come to have for that simple fluid such a regard as you, O reader, might not easily credit. And here each man chose a site where he would build his hut, and settle down, and marry perhaps, and even forget the sea; when Captain Shard having filled his tanks and barrels peremptorily ordered them to weigh anchor. There was much dissatisfaction, even some grumbling, but when a man has twice saved his fellows from death by the sheer freshness of his mind they come to have a respect for his judgment that is not shaken by trifles. It must be remembered that in the affair of the dropping of the wind and again when they ran out of water these men were at their wits' end: so was Shard on the last occasion, but that they did not know. All this Shard knew, and he chose this occasion to strengthen the reputation that he had in the minds of the men of that bad ship by explaining to them his motives, which usually he kept secret. The oasis he said must be a port of call for all the travellers within hundreds of miles: how many men did you see gathered together in any part of the world where there was a drop of whiskey to be had! And water here was rarer than whiskey in decent countries and, such was the peculiarity of the Arabs, even more precious. Another thing he pointed out to them, the Arabs were a singularly inquisitive people and if they came upon a ship in the desert they would probably talk about it; and the world having a wickedly malicious tongue would never construe in its proper light their difference with the English and Spanish fleets, but would merely side with the strong against the weak.

And the men sighed, and sang the capstan song and hoisted the anchor and yoked the oxen up, and away they went doing their steady knot, which nothing could increase. It may be thought strange that with all sail furled in dead calm and while the oxen rested they should have cast anchor at all. But custom is not easily overcome and long survives its use. Rather enquire how many such useless customs we ourselves preserve: the flaps for instance to pull up the tops of hunting-boots though the tops no longer pull up, the bows on our evening shoes that neither tie nor untie. They said they felt safer that way and there was an end of it.

Shard lay a course of South by West and they did ten knots that day, the next day they did seven or eight and Shard hove to. Here he intended to stop, they had huge supplies of fodder on board for the oxen, for his men he had a pig or so, plenty of poultry, several sacks of biscuits and ninety-eight oxen (for two were already eaten), and they were only twenty miles from water. Here he said they would stay till folks forgot their past, someone would invent something or some new thing would turn up to take folks' minds off them and the ships he had sunk: he forgot that there are men who are well paid to remember.

Half way between him and the oasis he established a little depot where he buried his water-barrels. As soon as a barrel was empty he sent half a dozen men to roll it by turns to the depot. This they would do at night, keeping hid by day, and next night they would push on to the oasis, fill the barrel and roll it back. Thus only ten miles away he soon had a store of water, unknown to the thirstiest native of Africa, from which he could safely replenish his tanks at will. He allowed his men to sing and even within reason to light fires. Those were jolly nights while the rum held out; sometimes they saw gazelles watching them curiously, sometimes a lion went by over the sand, the sound of his roar added to their sense of the security of their ship; all round them level, immense lay the Sahara: "This is better than an English prison," said Captain Shard.

And still the dead calm lasted, not even the sand whispered at night to little winds; and when the rum gave out and it looked like trouble, Shard reminded them what little use it had been to them when it was all they had and the oxen wouldn't look at it.

And the days wore on with singing, and even dancing at times, and at nights round a cautious fire in a hollow of sand with only one man on watch they told tales of the sea. It was all a relief after arduous watches and sleeping by the guns, a rest to strained nerves and eyes; and all agreed, for all that they missed their rum, that the best place for a ship like theirs was the land.

This was in Latitude 23 North, Longitude 4 East, where, as I have said, a ship's broadside was heard for the first time and the last. It happened this way.

They had been there several weeks and had eaten perhaps ten or a dozen oxen and all that while there had been no breath of wind and they had seen no one: when one morning about two bells when the crew were at breakfast the lookout man reported cavalry on the port side. Shard who had already surrounded his ship with sharpened stakes ordered all his men on board, the young trumpeter who prided himself on having picked up the ways of the land, sounded "Prepare to receive cavalry";. Shard sent a few men below with pikes to the lower port-holes, two more aloft with muskets, the rest to the guns, he changed the "grape" or "canister" with which the guns were loaded in case of surprise, for shot, cleared the decks, drew in ladders, and before the cavalry came within range everything was ready for them. The oxen were always yoked in order that Shard could manoeuvre his ship at a moment's notice.

When first sighted the cavalry were trotting but they were coming on now at a slow canter. Arabs in white robes on good horses. Shard estimated that there were two or three hundred of them. At sixty yards Shard opened with one gun, he had had the distance measured, but had never practised for fear of being heard at the oasis: the shot went high. The next one fell short and ricochetted over the Arabs' heads. Shard had the range then and by the time the ten remaining guns of his broadside were given the same elevation as that of his second gun the Arabs had come to the spot where the last shot pitched. The broadside hit the horses, mostly low, and ricochetted on amongst them; one cannon-ball striking a rock at the horses' feet shattered it and sent fragments flying amongst the Arabs with the peculiar scream of things set free by projectiles from their motionless harmless state, and the cannon-ball went on with them with a great howl, this shot alone killed three men.

"Very satisfactory," said Shard rubbing his chin. "Load with grape," he added sharply.

The broadside did not stop the Arabs nor even reduce their speed but they crowded in closer together as though for company in their time of danger, which they should not have done. They were four hundred yards off now, three hundred and fifty; and then the muskets began, for the two men in the crow's-nest had thirty loaded muskets besides a few pistols, the muskets all stood round them leaning against the rail; they picked them up and fired them one by one. Every shot told, but still the Arabs came on. They were galloping now. It took some time to load the guns in those days. Three hundred yards, two hundred and fifty, men dropping all the way, two hundred yards; Old Frank for all his one ear had terrible eyes; it was pistols now, they had fired all their muskets; a hundred and fifty; Shard had marked the fifties with little white stones. Old Frank and Bad Jack up aloft felt pretty uneasy when they saw the Arabs had come to that little white stone, they both missed their shots.

"All ready?" said Captain Shard.

"Aye, aye, sir," said Smerdrak.

"Right," said Captain Shard raising a finger.

A hundred and fifty yards is a bad range at which to be caught by grape (or "case" as we call it now), the gunners can hardly miss and the charge has time to spread. Shard estimated afterwards that he got thirty Arabs by that broadside alone and as many horses.

There were close on two hundred of them still on their horses, yet the broadside of grape had unsettled them, they surged round the ship but seemed doubtful what to do. They carried swords and scimitars in their hands, though most had strange long muskets slung behind them, a few unslung them and began firing wildly. They could not reach Shard's merry men with their swords. Had it not been for that broadside that took them when it did they might have climbed up from their horses and carried the bad ship by sheer force of numbers, but they would have had to have been very steady, and the broadside spoiled all that. Their best course was to have concentrated all their efforts in setting fire to the ship but this they did not attempt. Part of them swarmed all round the ship brandishing their swords and looking vainly for an easy entrance; perhaps they expected a door, they were not sea-faring people; but their leaders were evidently set on driving off the oxen not dreaming that the Desperate Lark had other means of travelling. And this to some extent they succeeded in doing. Thirty they drove off, cutting the traces, twenty they killed on the spot with their scimitars though the bow gun caught them twice as they did their work, and ten more were unluckily killed by Shard's bow gun. Before they could fire a third time from the bows they all galloped away, firing back at the oxen with their muskets and killing three more, and what troubled Shard more than the loss of his oxen was the way that they manoeuvred, galloping off just when the bow gun was ready and riding off by the port bow where the broadside could not get them, which seemed to him to show more knowledge of guns than they could have learned on that bright morning. What, thought Shard to himself, if they should bring big guns against the Desperate Lark! And the mere thought of it made him rail at Fate. But the merry men all cheered when they rode away. Shard had only twenty-two oxen left, and then a score or so of the Arabs dismounted while the rest rode further on leading their horses. And the dismounted men lay down on the port bow behind some rocks two hundred yards away and began to shoot at the oxen. Shard had just enough of them left to manoeuvre his ship with an effort and he turned his ship a few points to the starboard so as to get a broadside at the rocks. But grape was of no use here as the only way he could get an Arab was by hitting one of the rocks with shot behind which an Arab was lying, and the rocks were not easy to hit except by chance, and as often as he manoeuvred his ship the Arabs changed their ground. This went on all day while the mounted Arabs hovered out of range watching what Shard would do; and all the while the oxen were growing fewer, so good a mark were they, until only ten were left, and the ship could manoeuvre no longer. But then they all rode off.

The merry men were delighted, they calculated that one way and another they had unhorsed a hundred Arabs and on board there had been no more than one man wounded: Bad Jack had been hit in the wrist; probably by a bullet meant for the men at the guns, for the Arabs were firing high. They had captured a horse and had found quaint weapons on the bodies of the dead Arabs and an interesting kind of tobacco. It was evening now and they talked over the fight, made jokes about their luckier shots, smoked their new tobacco and sang; altogether it was the jolliest evening they'd had. But Shard alone on the quarter-deck paced to and fro pondering, brooding and wondering. He had chopped off Bad Jack's wounded hand and given him a hook out of store, for captain does doctor upon these occasions and Shard, who was ready for most things, kept half a dozen or so of neat new limbs, and of course a chopper. Bad Jack had gone below swearing a little and said he'd lie down for a bit, the men were smoking and singing on the sand, and Shard was there alone. The thought that troubled Shard was: What would the Arabs do? They did not look like men to go away for nothing. And at back of all his thoughts was one that reiterated guns, guns, guns. He argued with himself that they could not drag them all that way on the sand, that the Desperate Lark was not worth it, that they had given it up. Yet he knew in his heart that that was what they would do. He knew there were fortified towns in Africa, and as for its being worth it, he knew that there was no pleasant thing left now to those defeated men except revenge, and if the Desperate Lark had come over the sand why not guns? He knew that the ship could never hold out against guns and cavalry, a week perhaps, two weeks, even three: what difference did it make how long it was, and the men sang:

> Away we go,
> Oho, Oho, Oho,
> A drop of rum for you and me
> And the world's as round as the letter O
> And round it runs the sea.

A melancholy settled down on Shard. About sunset Lieutenant Smerdrak came up for orders. Shard ordered a trench to be dug along the port side of the ship. The men wanted to sing and grumbled at having to dig, especially as Shard never mentioned his fear of guns, but he fingered his pistols and in the end Shard had his way. No one on board could shoot like Captain Shard. That is often the way with captains of pirate ships, it is a difficult position to hold. Discipline is essential to those that have the right to fly the skull-and-cross-bones, and Shard was the man to enforce it. It was starlight by the time the trench was dug to the captain's satisfaction and the men that it was to protect when the worst came to the worst swore all the time as they dug. And when it was finished they clamoured to make a feast on some of the killed oxen, and this Shard let them do. And they lit a huge fire for the first time, burning abundant scrub, they thinking that Arabs daren't return, Shard knowing that concealment was now useless. All that night they feasted and sang, and Shard sat up in his chart-room making his plans.

When morning came they rigged up the cutter as they called the captured horse and told off her crew. As there were only two men that could ride at all these became the crew of the cutter. Spanish Dick and Bill the Boatswain were the two.

Shard's orders were that turn and turn about they should take command of the cutter and cruise about five miles off to the North East all the day but at night they were to come in. And they fitted the horse up with a flagstaff in front of the saddle so that they could signal from her, and carried an anchor behind for fear she should run away.

And as soon as Spanish Dick had ridden off Shard sent some men to roll all the barrels back from the depot where they were buried in the sand, with orders to watch the cutter all the time and, if she signalled, to return as fast as they could.

They buried the Arabs that day, removing their water-bottles and any provisions they had, and that night they got all the water-barrels in, and for days nothing happened. One event of extraordinary importance did indeed occur, the wind got up one day, but it was due South, and as the oasis lay to the North of them and beyond that

they might pick up the camel track Shard
decided to stay where he was. If it had
looked to him like lasting Shard might have
hoisted sail but it dropped at evening as he
knew it would, and in any case it was not
the wind he wanted. And more days went
by, two weeks without a breeze. The dead
oxen would not keep and they had had to
kill three more, there were only seven left
now.

Never before had the men been so long
without rum. And Captain Shard had
doubled the watch besides making two more
men sleep at the guns. They had tired of
their simple games, and most of their songs,
and their tales that were never true were no
longer new. And then one day the monotony of the desert came down upon them.

There is a fascination in the Sahara, a day
there is delightful, a week is pleasant, a fortnight is a matter of opinion, but it was running into months. The men were perfectly
polite but the boatswain wanted to know
when Shard thought of moving on. It was
an unreasonable question to ask of the captain of any ship in a dead calm in a desert,
but Shard said he would set a course and let

him know in a day or two. And a day or two went by over the monotony of the Sahara, who for monotony is unequalled by all the parts of the earth. Great marshes cannot equal it, nor plains of grass nor the sea, the Sahara alone lies unaltered by the seasons, she has no altering surface, no flowers to fade or grow, year in year out she is changeless for hundreds and hundreds of miles. And the boatswain came again and took off his cap and asked Captain Shard to be so kind as to tell them about his new course. Shard said he meant to stay until they had eaten three more of the oxen as they could only take three of them in the hold, there were only six left now. But what if there was no wind, the boatswain said. And at that moment the faintest breeze from the North ruffled the boatswain's forelock as he stood with his cap in his hand.

"Don't talk about the wind to *me*," said Captain Shard: and Bill was a little frightened for Shard's mother had been a gipsy.

But it was only a breeze astray, a trick of the Sahara. And another week went by and they ate two more oxen.

They obeyed Captain Shard ostentatiously now but they wore ominous looks. Bill came again and Shard answered him in Romany.

Things were like this one hot Sahara morning when the cutter signalled. The lookout man told Shard and Shard read the message, "Cavalry astern" it read, and then a little later she signalled,"With guns."

"Ah," said Captain Shard.

One ray of hope Shard had; the flags on the cutter fluttered. For the first time for five weeks a light breeze blew from the North, very light, you hardly felt it. Spanish Dick rode in and anchored his horse to starboard and the cavalry came on slowly from the port.

Not till the afternoon did they come in sight, and all the while that little breeze was blowing.

"One knot," said Shard at noon. "Two knots," he said at six bells and still it grew and the Arabs trotted nearer. By five o'clock the merry men of the bad ship Desperate Lark could make out twelve long old-fashioned guns on low wheeled carts dragged by horses and what looked like lighter guns carried on camels. The wind was blowing a little stronger now. "Shall we hoist sail, sir?" said Bill.

"Not yet," said Shard.

By six o'clock the Arabs were just outside the range of cannon and there they halted. Then followed an anxious hour or so, but the Arabs came no nearer. They evidently meant to wait till dark to bring their guns up. Probably they intended to dig a gun epaulment from which they could safely pound away at the ship.

"We could do three knots," said Shard half to himself as he was walking up and down his quarter-deck with very fast short paces. And then the sun set and they heard the Arabs praying and Shard's merry men cursed at the top of their voices to show that they were as good men as they.

The Arabs had come no nearer, waiting for night. They did not know how Shard was longing for it too, he was gritting his teeth and sighing for it, he even would have prayed, but that he feared that it might remind Heaven of him and his merry men.

Night came and the stars. "Hoist sail," said Shard. The men sprang to their places, they had had enough of that silent lonely spot. They took the oxen on board and let the great sails down, and like a lover coming from over sea, long dreamed of, long expected, like a lost friend seen again after many years, the North wind came into the pirates' sails. And before Shard could stop it a ringing English cheer went away to the wondering Arabs.

They started off at three knots and soon they might have done four but Shard would not risk it at night. All night the wind held good, and doing three knots from ten to four they were far out of sight of the Arabs when daylight came. And then Shard hoisted more sail and they did four knots and by eight bells they were doing four and a half. The spirits of those volatile men rose high, and discipline became perfect. So long as there was wind in the sails and water in the tanks Captain Shard felt safe at least from mutiny. Great men can only be overthrown while their fortunes are at their lowest. Having failed to depose Shard when his plans were open to criticism and he himself scarce knew what to do next it was hardly likely they could do it now;

and whatever we think of his past and his way of living we cannot deny that Shard was among the great men of the world.

Of defeat by the Arabs he did not feel so sure. It was useless to try to cover his tracks even if he had had time, the Arab cavalry could have picked them up anywhere. And he was afraid of their camels with those light guns on board, he had heard they could do seven knots and keep it up most of the day and if as much as one shot struck the mainmast . . . . and Shard taking his mind off useless fears worked out on his chart when the Arabs were likely to overtake them. He told his men that the wind would hold good for a week, and, gipsy or no, he certainly knew as much about the wind as is good for a sailor to know.

Alone in his chart-room he worked it out like this, mark two hours to the good for surprise and finding the tracks and delay in starting, say three hours if the guns were mounted in their epaulments, then the Arabs should start at seven. Supposing the camels go twelve hours a day at seven knots they would do eighty-four knots a day, while Shard doing three knots from ten to four, and four knots the rest of the time, was doing ninety and actually gaining. But when it came to it he wouldn't risk more than two knots at night while the enemy were out of sight, for he rightly regarded anything more than that as dangerous when sailing on land at night, so he too did eighty-four knots a day. It was a pretty race. I have not troubled to see if Shard added up his figures wrongly or if he under-rated the pace of camels, but whatever it was the Arabs gained slightly, for on the fourth day Spanish Jack, five knots astern on what they called the cutter, sighted the camels a very long way off and signalled the fact to Shard They had left their cavalry behind as Shard supposed they would. The wind held good, they had still two oxen left and could always eat their "cutter", and they had a fair, though not ample, supply of water, but the appearance of the Arabs was a blow to Shard for it showed him that there was no getting away from them, and of all things he dreaded guns. He made light of it to the men: said they would sink the lot before they had been in action half an hour: yet he feared that once the guns came up it was only a question of time before his rigging was cut or his steering gear disabled.

One point the Desperate Lark scored over the Arabs and a very good one too, darkness fell just before they could have sighted her and now Shard used the lantern ahead as he dared not do on the first night when the Arabs were close, and with the help of it managed to do three knots.   The Arabs encamped in the evening and the Desperate Lark gained twenty knots.   But the next evening they appeared again and this time they saw the sails of the Desperate Lark.

On the sixth day they were close.   On the seventh they were closer.   And then, a line of verdure across their bows, Shard saw the Niger River.

Whether he knew that for a thousand miles it rolled its course through forest, whether he even knew that it was there at all; what his plans were, or whether he lived from day to day like a man whose days are numbered he never told his men.   Nor can I get an indication on this point from the talk that I hear from sailors in their cups in a certain tavern I know of.   His face was expressionless, his mouth shut, and he held his ship to her course. That evening they were up to the edge of the tree trunks and the Arabs camped and waited ten knots astern and the wind had sunk a little.

There Shard anchored a little before sunset and landed at once. At first he explored the forest a little on foot. Then he sent for Spanish Dick. They had slung the cutter on board some days ago when they found she could not keep up. Shard could not ride but he sent for Spanish Dick and told him he must take him as a passenger. So Spanish Dick slung him in front of the saddle "before the mast" as Shard called it, for they still carried a mast on the front of the saddle, and away they galloped together. "Rough weather," said Shard, but he surveyed the forest as he went and the long and short of it was he found a place where the forest was less than half a mile thick and the Desperate Lark might get through: but twenty trees must be cut. Shard marked the trees himself, sent Spanish Dick right back to watch the Arabs and turned the whole of his crew on to those twenty trees. It was a frightful risk, the Desperate Lark was empty, with an enemy no more than ten knots astern, but it was a moment for bold measures and Shard took the chance of being left without his ship in the heart of Africa in the hope of being repaid by escaping altogether.

The men worked all night on those twenty trees, those that had no axes bored with bradawls and blasted, and then relieved those that had.

Shard was indefatigable, he went from tree to tree showing exactly what way every one was to fall, and what was to be done with them when they were down. Some had to be cut down because their branches would get in the way of the masts, others because their trunks would be in the way of the wheels; in the case of the last the stumps had to be made smooth and low with saws and perhaps a bit of the trunk sawn off and rolled away. This was the hardest work they had. And they were all large trees, on the other hand had they been small there would have been many more of them and they could not have sailed in and out, sometimes for hundreds of yards, without cutting any at all: and all this Shard calculated on doing if only there was time.

The light before dawn came and it looked as if they would never do it at all. And then dawn came and it was all done but one tree, the hard part of the work had all been done in the night and a sort of final rush cleared everything up except that one huge tree. And then the cutter signalled the Arabs were moving. At dawn they had prayed, and now they had struck their camp. Shard at once ordered all his men to the ship except ten whom he left at the tree, they had some way to go and the Arabs had been moving some ten minutes before they got there. Shard took in the cutter which wasted five minutes, hoisted sail short-handed and that took five minutes more, and slowly got under way.

The wind was dropping still and by the time the Desperate Lark had come to the edge of that part of the forest through which Shard had laid his course the Arabs were no more than five knots away. He had sailed East half a mile, which he ought to have done overnight so as to be ready, but he could not spare time or thought or men away from those twenty trees. Then Shard turned into the forest and the Arabs were dead astern. They hurried when they saw the Desperate Lark enter the forest.

"Doing ten knots," said Shard as he watched them from the deck. The Desperate Lark was doing no more than a knot and a half for the wind was weak under the lee of the trees. Yet all went well for a while. The big tree had just come down some way ahead, and the ten men were sawing bits off the trunk.

And then Shard saw a branch that he had not marked on the chart, it would just catch the top of the mainmast. He anchored at once and sent a hand aloft who sawed it half way through and did the rest with a pistol, and now the Arabs were only three knots astern. For a quarter of a mile Shard steered them through the forest till they came to the ten men and that bad big tree, another foot had yet to come off one corner of the stump for the wheels had to pass over it. Shard turned all hands on to the stump and it was then that the Arabs came within shot. But they had to unpack their gun. And before they had it mounted Shard was away. If they had charged things might have been different. When they saw the

Desperate Lark under way again the Arabs came on to within three hundred yards and there they mounted two guns. Shard watched them along his stern gun but would not fire. They were six hundred yards away before the Arabs could fire and then they fired too soon and both guns missed. And Shard and his merry men saw clear water only ten fathoms ahead. Then Shard loaded his stern gun with canister instead of shot and at the same moment the Arabs charged on their camels; they came galloping down through the forest waving long lances. Shard left the steering to Smerdrak and stood by the stern gun, the Arabs were within fifty yards and still Shard did not fire; he had most of his men in the stern with muskets beside him. Those lances carried on camels were altogether different from swords in the hands of horsemen, they could reach the men on deck. The men could see the horrible barbs on the lance-heads, they were almost at their faces when Shard fired, and at the same moment the Desperate Lark with her dry and sun-cracked keel in air on the high bank of the Niger fell forward like a diver. The gun went off through the tree-tops, a wave came over the bows and swept the stern, the Desperate Lark wriggled and righted herself, she was back in her element.

The merry men looked at the wet decks and at their dripping clothes. "Water," they said almost wonderingly.

The Arabs followed a little way through the forest but when they saw that they had to face a broadside instead of one stern gun and perceived that a ship afloat is less vulnerable to cavalry even than when on shore, they abandoned ideas of revenge, and comforted themselves with a text out of their sacred book which tells how in other days and other places our enemies shall suffer even as we desire.

For a thousand miles with the flow of the Niger and the help of occasional winds, the Desperate Lark moved seawards. At first he sweeps East a little and then Southwards, till you come to Akassa and the open sea.

I will not tell you how they caught fish and ducks, raided a village here and there and at last came to Akassa, for I have said much already of Captain Shard. Imagine them drawing nearer and nearer the sea, bad men all, and yet with a feeling for something where we feel for our king, our country or our home, a feeling for something that burned in them not less ardently than our feelings in us, and that something the sea. Imagine them nearing it till sea birds appeared and they fancied they felt sea breezes and all sang songs again that they had not sung for weeks. Imagine them heaving at last on the salt Atlantic again.

I have said much already of Captain Shard and I fear lest I shall weary you, O my reader, if I tell you any more of so bad a man. I too at the top of a tower all alone am weary.

And yet it is right that such a tale should be told. A journey almost due South from near Algiers to Akassa in a ship that we should call no more than a yacht. Let it be a stimulus to younger men.

GUARANTEE TO THE READER

Since writing down for your benefit, O my reader, all this long tale that I heard in the tavern by the sea I have travelled in Algeria and Tunisia as well as in the Desert.

Much that I saw in those countries seems to throw doubt on the tale that the sailor told me. To begin with the Desert does not come within hundreds of miles of the coast and there are more mountains to cross than you would suppose, the Atlas mountains in particular. It is just possible Shard might have got through by El Cantara, following the camel road which is many centuries old; or he may have gone by Algiers and Bou Saada and through the mountain pass El Finita Dem, though that is a bad enough way for camels to go (let alone bullocks with a ship) for which reason the Arabs call it Finita Dem — the Path of Blood.

I should not have ventured to give this story the publicity of print had the sailor been sober when he told it, for fear that he should have deceived you, O my reader; but this was never the case with him as I took good care to ensure: "in vino veritas" is a sound old proverb, and I never had cause to doubt his word unless that proverb lies.

If it should prove that he has deceived me, let it pass; but if he has been the means of deceiving you there are little things about

him that I know, the common gossip of that
ancient tavern whose leaded bottle-glass
windows watch the sea, which I will tell at
once to every judge of my acquaintance,
and it will be a pretty race to see which of
them will hang him.

Meanwhile, O my reader, believe the
story, resting assured that if you are taken
in the thing shall be a matter for the hang-
man.

A Tale of
the Equator

e who is Sultan so remote to the East that his dominions were deemed fabulous in Babylon, whose name is a by-word for distance to-day in the streets of Bagdad, whose capital bearded travellers invoke by name in the gate at evening to gather hearers to their tales when the smoke of tobacco arises, dice rattle and taverns shine; even he in that very city made mandate, and said: "Let there be brought hither all my learned men that they may come before me and rejoice my heart with learning."

Men ran and clarions sounded, and it was so that there came before the Sultan all of his learned men. And many were found wanting. But of those that were able to say acceptable things, ever after to be named The Fortunate, one said that to the South of the Earth lay a Land — said Land was crowned with lotus — where it was summer in our winter days and where it was winter in summer.

And when the Sultan of those most distant lands knew that the Creator of All had contrived a device so vastly to his delight his merriment knew no bounds. On a sudden he spake and said, and this was the gist of his saying, that upon that line of boundary or limit that divided the North from the South a palace be made, where in the Northern courts should summer be, while in the South was winter; so should he move from court to court according to his mood, and dally with the summer in the morning and spend the noon with snow. So the Sultan's poets were sent for and bade to tell of that city, foreseeing its splendour far away to the South and in the future of time; and some were found fortunate. And of those that were found fortunate and were crowned with flowers none earned more easily the Sultan's smile (on which long days depended) than he that foreseeing the city spake of it thus:

"In seven years and seven days, O Prop of Heaven, shall thy builders build it, thy palace that is neither North nor South, where neither summer nor winter is sole lord of the hours. White I see it, very vast, as a city, very fair, as a woman, Earth's wonder, with many windows, with thy princesses peering out at twilight; yea, I behold the bliss of the gold balconies, and hear a rustling down long galleries and the doves' coo upon its sculptured eaves. O Prop of Heaven, would that so fair a city were built by thine ancient sires, the children of the sun, that so might all men see it even to-day, and not the poets only, whose vision sees it so far away to the South and in the future of time.

"O King of the Years, it shall stand midmost on that line that divideth equally the North from the South and that parteth the seasons asunder as with a screen. On the Northern side when summer is in the North thy silken guards shall pace by dazzling walls while thy spearsmen clad in furs go round the South. But at the hour of noon in the midmost day of the year thy chamberlain shall go down from his high place and into the midmost court, and men with trumpets shall go down behind him, and he shall utter a great cry at noon, and the men with trumpets shall cause their trumpets to blare, and the spearsmen clad in furs shall march to the North and thy silken guard shall take their place in the South, and summer shall leave the North and go to the South, and all the swallows shall rise and follow after. And alone in thine inner courts shall no change be, for they shall lie narrowly along that line that parteth the seasons in sunder and divideth the North from the South, and thy long gardens shall lie under them.

"And in thy gardens shall spring always be, for spring lies ever at the marge of summer; and autumn also shall always tint thy gardens, for autumn always flares at winter's edge, and those gardens shall lie apart between winter and summer. And there shall be orchards in thy garden, too, with all the burden of autumn on their boughs and all the blossom of spring.

"Yea, I behold this palace, for we see future things; I see its white wall shine in the huge glare of midsummer, and the lizards lying along it motionless in the sun, and men asleep in the noonday, and the butterflies floating by, and birds of radiant plumage chasing marvellous moths; far off the forest and great orchids glorying there, and iridescent insects dancing round in the light. I see the wall upon the other side; the snow has come upon the battlements, the icicles have fringed them like frozen beards, a wild wind blowing out of lonely places and crying to the cold fields as it blows has sent the snowdrifts higher than the buttresses; they that look out through windows on that side of thy palace see the wild geese flying low and all the birds of the winter, going by swift in packs beat low by the bitter wind, and the clouds above them are black, for it is midwinter there; while in thine other courts the fountains tinkle, falling on marble warmed by the fire of the summer sun.

"Such, O King of the Years, shall thy palace be, and its name shall be Erlathdronion, Earth's Wonder; and thy wisdom shall bid thine architects build at once, that all may see what as yet the poets see only, and that prophecy be fulfilled."

And when the poet ceased the Sultan

spake, and said, as all men hearkened with bent heads:

"It will be unnecessary for my builders to build this palace, Erlathdronion, Earth's Wonder, for in hearing thee we have drunk already its pleasures."

And the poet went forth from the Presence and dreamed a new thing.

．　　•　　•　　•　　•　　•

A Narrow Escape

I t was underground.

In that dank cavern down below Belgrave Square the walls were dripping. But what was that to the magician? It was secrecy that he needed, not dryness. There he pondered upon the trend of events, shaped destinies and concocted magical brews.

For the last few years the serenity of his ponderings had been disturbed by the noise of the motor-bus; while to his keen ears there came the earthquake-rumble, far off, of the train in the tube, going down Sloane Street; and when he heard of the world above his head was not to its credit.

He decided one evening over his evil pipe, down there in his dank chamber, that London had lived long enough, had abused its opportunities, had gone too far, in fine, with its civilisation. And so he decided to wreck it.

Therefore he beckoned up his acolyte from the weedy end of the cavern, and, "Bring me," he said, "the heart of the toad that dwelleth in Arabia and by the mountains of Bethany." The acolyte slipped away by the hidden door, leaving that grim old man with his frightful pipe, and whither he went who knows but the gipsy people, or by what path he returned; but within a year he stood in the cavern again, slipping secretly in by the trap while the old man smoked, and he brought with him a little fleshy thing that rotted in a casket of pure gold.

"What is it?" the old man croaked.

"It is," said the acolyte, "the heart of the toad that dwelt once in Arabia and by the mountains of Bethany."

The old man's crooked fingers closed on it, and he blessed the acolyte with his rasping voice and claw-like hand uplifted; the motor-bus rumbled above on its endless journey; far off the train shook Sloane Street.

"Come," said the old magician, "it is time." And there and then they left the weedy cavern, the acolyte carrying cauldron, gold poker and all things needful, and went abroad in the light. And very wonderful the old man looked in his silks.

Their goal was the outskirts of London; the old man strode in front and the acolyte ran behind him, and there was something magical in the old man's stride alone, without his wonderful dress, the cauldron and wand, the hurrying acolyte and the small gold poker.

Little boys jeered till they caught the old man's eye. So there went on through London this strange procession of two, too swift for any to follow. Things seemed worse up there than they did in the cavern, and the further they got on their way towards London's outskirts the worse London got. "It is time," said the old man, "surely."

And so they came at last to London's edge and a small hill watching it with a mournful look. It was so mean that the acolyte longed for the cavern, dank though it was and full of terrible sayings that the old man said when he slept.

161

They climbed the hill and put the cauldron down, and put there in the necessary things, and lit a fire of herbs that no chemist will sell nor decent gardener grow, and stirred the cauldron with the golden poker. The magician retired a little apart and muttered, then he strode back to the cauldron and, all being ready, suddenly opened the casket and let the fleshy thing fall in to boil.

Then he made spells, then he flung up his arms; the fumes from the cauldron entering in at his mind he said raging things that he had not known before and runes that were dreadful (the acolyte screamed); there he cursed London from fog to loam-pit, from zenith to the abyss, motor-bus, factory, shop, parliament, people. "Let them all perish," he said, "and London pass away, tram lines and bricks and pavement, the usurpers too long of the fields, let them all pass away and the wild hares come back, blackberry and briar-rose."

"Let it pass," he said, "pass now, pass utterly."

In the momentary silence the old man coughed, then waited with eager eyes; and the long long hum of London hummed as it always has since first the reed-huts were set up by the river, changing its note at times but always humming, louder now than it was in years gone by, but humming night and day though its voice be cracked with age; so it hummed on.

And the old man turned him round to his trembling acolyte and terribly said as he sank into the earth: "YOU HAVE NOT BROUGHT ME THE HEART OF THE TOAD THAT DWELLETH IN ARABIA NOR BY THE MOUNTAINS OF BETHANY!"

The Watch-tower

I sat one April in Provence on a small hill above an ancient town that Goth and Vandal as yet have forborne to "bring up to date."

On the hill was an old worn castle with a watch-tower, and a well with narrow steps and water in it still.

The watch-tower, staring South with neglected windows, faced a broad valley full of the pleasant twilight and the hum of evening things: it saw the fires of wanderers blink from the hills, beyond them the long forest black with pines, one star appearing, and darkness settling slowly down on Var.

Sitting there listening to the green frogs croaking, hearing far voices clearly but all transmuted by evening, watching the windows in the little town glimmering one by one, and seeing the gloaming dwindle solemnly into night, a great many things fell from mind that seem important by day, and evening in their place planted strange fancies.

Little winds had arisen and were whispering to and fro, it grew cold, and I was about to descend the hill, when I heard a voice behind me saying, "Beware, beware."

So much the voice appeared a part of the evening that I did not turn round at first; it was like voices that one hears in sleep and thinks to be of one's dream. And the word was monotonously repeated, in French.

When I turned round I saw an old man with a horn. He had a white beard marvellously long, and still went on saying slowly, "Beware, beware." He had clearly just come from the tower by which he stood, though I had heard no footfall. Had a man come stealthily upon me at such an hour and in so lonesome a place I had certainly felt surprised; but I saw almost at once that he was a spirit, and he seemed with his uncouth horn and his long white beard and that noiseless step of his to be so native to that time and place that I spoke to him as one does to some fellow-traveller who asks you if you mind having the window up.

I asked him what there was to beware of.

"Of what should a town beware," he said, "but the Saracens?"

"Saracens?" I said.

"Yes, Saracens, Saracens," he answered and brandished his horn.

"And who are you?" I said.

"I, I am the spirit of the tower," he said.

When I asked him how he came by so human an aspect and was so unlike the material tower beside him he told me that the lives of all the watchers who had ever held the horn in the tower there had gone to make the spirit of the tower. "It takes a hundred lives," he said. "None hold the horn of late and men neglect the tower. When the walls are in ill repair the Saracens come: it was ever so."

"The Saracens don't come nowadays," I said.

But he was gazing past me watching, and did not seem to heed me.

"They will run down those hills," he said, pointing away to the South, "out of the woods about nightfall, and I shall blow my horn. The people will all come up from the town to the tower again; but the loopholes are in very ill repair."

"We never hear of the Saracens now," I said.

"Hear of the Saracens!" the old spirit said. "Hear of the Saracens! They slip one evening out of that forest, in the long white robes that they wear, and I blow my horn. That is the first that anyone ever hears of the Saracens."

"I mean," I said, "that they never come at all. They cannot come and men fear other things." For I thought the old spirit might rest if he knew that the Saracens can never come again. But he said, "There is nothing in the world to fear but the Saracens. Nothing else matters. How can men fear other things?"

Then I explained, so that he might have rest, and told him how all Europe, and in particular France, had terrible engines of war, both on land and sea; and how the Saracens had not these terrible engines either on sea or land, and so could by no means cross the Mediterranean or escape destruction on shore even though they

167

should come there. I alluded to the European railways that could move armies night and day faster than horses could gallop. And when as well as I could I had explained all, he answered, "In time all these things pass away and then there will still be the Saracens."

And then I said, "There has not been a Saracen either in France or Spain for over four hundred years."

And he said, "The Saracens! You do not know their cunning. That was ever the way of the Saracens. They do not come for a while, no not they, for a long while, and then one day they come."

And peering southwards, but not seeing clearly because of the rising mist, he silently moved to his tower and up its broken steps.

How Plash-Goo
Came to the Land
of None's Desire

**I**n a thatched cottage of enormous size, so vast that we might consider it a palace, but only a cottage in the style of its building, its timbers and the nature of its interior, there lived Plash-Goo.

Plash-Goo was of the children of the giants, whose sire was Uph. And the lineage of Uph had dwindled in bulk for the last five hundred years, till the giants were now no more than fifteen foot high; but Uph ate elephants which he caught with his hands.

Now on the tops of the mountains above the house of Plash-Goo, for Plash-Goo lived in the plains, there dwelt the dwarf whose name was Lrippity-Kang.

And the dwarf used to walk at evening on the edge of the tops of the mountains, and would walk up and down along it, and was squat and ugly and hairy, and was plainly seen of Plash-Goo.

And for many weeks the giant had suffered the sight of him, but at length grew irked at the sight (as men are by little things), and could not sleep of a night and lost his taste for pigs. And at last there came the day, as anyone might have known, when Plash-Goo shouldered his club and went up to look for the dwarf.

And the dwarf though briefly squat was broader than may be dreamed, beyond all breadth of man, and stronger than men may know; strength in its very essence dwelt in that little frame, as a spark in the heart of a flint: but to Plash-Goo he was no more than mis-shapen, bearded and squat, a thing that dared to defy all natural laws by being more broad than long.

When Plash-Goo came to the mountain he cast his chimahalk down (for so he named the club of his heart's desire) lest the dwarf should defy him with nimbleness; and stepped towards Lrippity-Kang with gripping hands, who stopped in his mountainous walk without a word, and swung round his hideous breadth to confront Plash-Goo.

Already then Plash-Goo in the deeps of his mind had seen himself seize the dwarf in one large hand and hurl him with his beard and his hated breadth sheer down the precipice that dropped away from that very place to the land of None's Desire. Yet it was otherwise that Fate would have it. For the dwarf parried with his little arms the grip of those monstrous hands, and gradually working along the enormous limbs came at length to the giant's body where by dwarfish cunning he obtained a grip; and turning Plash-Goo about, as a spider does some great fly, till his little grip was suitable to his purpose, he suddenly lifted the giant over his head. Slowly at first, by the edge of that precipice whose base sheer distance hid, he swung his giant victim round his head, but soon faster and faster; and at last when Plash-Goo was streaming round the hated breadth of the dwarf and the no less hated beard was flapping in the wind, Lrippity-Kang let go. Plash-Goo shot over the edge and for some way further, out

towards Space, like a stone; then he began
to fall. It was long before he believed and
truly knew that this was really he that fell
from this mountain, for we do not associate
such dooms with ourselves; but when he had
fallen for some while through the evening
and saw below him, where there had been
nothing to see, or *began* to see, the glimmer
of tiny fields, then his optimism departed;
till later on when the fields were greener and
larger he saw that this was indeed (and
growing now terribly nearer) that very land
to which he had destined the dwarf.

At last he saw it unmistakable, close, with
its grim houses and its dreadful ways, and
its green fields shining in the light of the
evening. His cloak was streaming from
him in whistling shreds.

So Plash-Goo came to the Land of None's
Desire.

The Three
Sailors' Gamble

itting some years ago in the ancient tavern at Over, one afternoon in Spring, I was waiting, as was my custom, for something strange to happen. In this I was not always disappointed for the very curious leaded panes of that tavern, facing the sea, let a light into the low-ceilinged room so mysterious, particularly at evening, that it somehow seemed to affect the events within. Be that as it may, I have seen strange things in that tavern and heard stranger things told.

And as I sat there three sailors entered the tavern, just back, as they said, from sea, and come with sunburned skins from a very long voyage to the South; and one of them had a board and chessmen under his arm, and they were complaining that they could find no one who knew how to play chess. This was the year that the Tournament was in England. And a little dark man at a table in a corner of the room, drinking sugar and water, asked them why they wished to play chess; and they said that they would play any man for a pound. They opened their box of chessmen then, a cheap and nasty set, and the man refused to play with such uncouth pieces, and the sailors suggested that perhaps he could find better ones; and in the end he went round to his lodgings near by and brought his own, and then they sat down to play for a pound a side. It was a consultation game on the part of the sailors, they said all three must play.

Well, the little dark man turned out to be Stavlokratz.

Of course he was fabulously poor, and the sovereign meant more to him than it did to the sailors, but he didn't seem keen to play, it was the sailors that insisted; he had made the badness of the sailors' chessmen an excuse for not playing at all, but the sailors had over-ruled that, and then he told them straight out who he was, and the sailors had never heard of Stavlokratz.

Well, no more was said after that. Stavlokratz said no more, either because he did not wish to boast or because he was huffed that they did not know who he was. And I saw no reason to enlighten the sailors about him; if he took their pound they had brought it on themselves, and my boundless admiration for his genius made me feel that he deserved whatever might come his way. He had not asked to play, they had named the stakes, he had warned them, and gave them first move; there was nothing unfair about Stavlokratz.

I had never seen Stavlokratz before, but I had played over nearly every one of his games in the World Championship for the last three or four years; he was always of course the model chosen by students. Only young chess-players can appreciate my delight at seeing him play first hand.

Well, the sailors used to lower their heads almost as low as the table and mutter together before every move, but they muttered so low that you could not hear what they planned.

They lost three pawns almost straight off, then a knight, and shortly after a bishop; they were playing in fact the famous Three Sailors' Gambit.

Stavlokratz was playing with the easy confidence that they say was usual with him, when suddenly at about the thirteenth move I saw him look surprised; he leaned forward and looked at the board and then at the sailors, but he learned nothing from their vacant faces; he looked back at the board again.

He moved more deliberately after that; the sailors lost two more pawns, Stavlokratz had lost nothing as yet. He looked at me I thought almost irritably, as though something would happen that he wished I was not there to see. I believed at first he had qualms about taking the sailors' pound, until it dawned on me that he might lose the game; I saw that possibility in his face, not on the board, for the game had become almost incomprehensible to me. I cannot describe my astonishment. And a few moves later Stavlokratz resigned.

The sailors showed no more elation than if they had won some game with greasy cards, playing amongst themselves.

Stavlokratz asked them where they got their opening. "We kind of thought of it," said one. "It just come into our heads like," said another. He asked them questions about the ports they had touched at. He evidently thought as I did myself that they had learned their extraordinary gambit, perhaps in some old dependancy of Spain, from some young master of chess whose fame had not reached Europe. He was very eager to find who this man could be, for neither of us imagined that those sailors had invented it, nor would anyone who had seen them. But he got no information from the sailors.

Stavlokratz could very ill afford the loss of a pound. He offered to play them again for the same stakes. The sailors began to set up the white pieces. Stavlokratz pointed out that it was his turn for first move. The sailors agreed but continued to set up the white pieces and sat with the white before them waiting for him to move. It was a trivial incident, but it revealed to Stavlokratz and myself that none of these sailors was aware that white always moves first.

Stavlokratz played on them his own opening, reasoning of course that as they had
never heard of Stavlokratz they would not
know of his opening; and with probably a
very good hope of getting back his pound
he played the fifth variation with its tricky
seventh move, at least so he intended, but
it turned to a variation unknown to the
students of Stavlokratz.

Throughout this game I watched the
sailors closely, and I became sure, as only
an attentive watcher can be, that the one
on their left, Jim Bunion, did not even know
the moves.

When I had made up my mind about this
I watched only the other two, Adam Bailey
and Bill Sloggs, trying to make out which
was the master mind; and for a long while
I could not. And then I heard Adam
Bailey mutter six words, the only words I
heard throughout the game, of all their con-
sultations, "No, him with the horse's head."
And I decided that Adam Bailey did not
know what a knight was, though of course
he might have been explaining things to
Bill Sloggs, but it did not sound like that;
so that left Bill Sloggs. I watched Bill

Sloggs after that with a certain wonder; he was no more intellectual than the others to look at, though rather more forceful perhaps. Poor old Stavlokratz was beaten again.

Well, in the end I paid for Stavlokratz, and tried to get a game with Bill Sloggs alone, but this he would not agree to, it must be all three or none: and then I went back with Stavlokratz to his lodgings. He very kindly gave me a game: of course it did not last long but I am more proud of having been beaten by Stavlokratz than of any game that I have ever won. And then we talked for an hour about the sailors, and neither of us could make head or tale of them. I told him what I had noticed about Jim Bunion and Adam Bailey, and he agreed with me that Bill Sloggs was the man, though as to how he had come by that gambit or that variation of Stavlokratz's own opening he had no theory.

I had the sailors' address which was that tavern as much as anywhere, and they were to be there all that evening. As evening drew in I went back to the tavern, and found there still the three sailors. And I offered Bill Sloggs two pounds for a game with him alone and he refused, but in the end he played me for a drink. And then I found that he had not heard of the "en passant" rule, and believed that the fact of checking the king prevented him from castling, and did not know that a player can have two or more queens on the board at the same time if he queens his pawns, or that a pawn could ever become a knight; and he made as many of the stock mistakes as he had time for in a short game, which I won. I thought that I should have got at the secret then, but his mates who had sat scowling all the while in the corner came up and interfered. It was a breach of their compact apparently for one to play chess by himself, at any rate they seemed angry. So I left the tavern then and came back again next day, and the next day and the day after, and often saw the three sailors, but none were in a communicative mood. I had got Stavlokratz to keep away, and they could get no one to play chess with at a pound a side, and I would not play with them unless they told me the secret.

And then one evening I found Jim Bunion

drunk, yet not so drunk as he wished, for the two pounds were spent; and I gave him very nearly a tumbler of whiskey, or what passed for whiskey in that tavern at Over, and he told me the secret at once. I had given the others some whiskey to keep them quiet, and later on in the evening they must have gone out, but Jim Bunion stayed with me by a little table leaning across it and talking low, right into my face, his breath smelling all the while of what passed for whiskey.

The wind was blowing outside as it does on bad nights in November, coming up with moans from the South, towards which the tavern faced with all its leaded panes, so that none but I was able to hear his voice as Jim Bunion gave up his secret.

They had sailed for years, he told me, with Bill Snyth; and on their last voyage home Bill Snyth had died. And he was buried at sea. Just the other side of the line they buried him, and his pals divided his kit, and these three got his crystal that only they knew he had, which Bill got one night in Cuba. They played chess with the crystal.

And he was going on to tell me about that night in Cuba when Bill had bought the crystal from the stranger, how some folks might think that they had seen thunderstorms, but let them go and listen to that one that thundered in Cuba when Bill was buying his crystal and they'd find that they didn't know what thunder was. But then I interrupted him, unfortunately perhaps, for it broke the thread of his tale and set him rambling a while, and cursing other people and talking of other lands, China, Port Said and Spain: but I brought him back to Cuba agnin in the end. I asked him how they could play chess with a crystal; and he said that you looked at the board and looked at the crystal and there was the game in the crystal the same as it was on the board, with all the odd little pieces looking just the same though smaller, horses' heads and whatnots; and as soon as the other man moved the move came out in the crystal, and then your move appeared after it, and all you had to do was to make it on the board. If you didn't make the move that you saw in the crystal things got very bad in it, everything horribly mixed and moving about rapidly, and scowling and making the same move over and over again, and the crystal getting cloudier and cloudier; it was best to take one's eyes away from it then, or one dreamt about it afterwards, and the foul little pieces came and cursed you in your sleep and moved about all night with their crooked moves.

I thought then that, drunk though he was, he was not telling the truth, and I promised to show him to people who played chess all their lives so that he and his mates could get a pound whenever they liked, and I promised not to reveal his secret even to Stavlokratz, if only he would tell me all the truth; and this promise I have kept till long after the three sailors have lost their secret. I told him straight out that I did not believe in the crystal. Well, Jim Bunion leaned forward then, even further across the table, and swore he had seen the man from whom Bill had bought the crystal and that he was one to whom anything was possible. To begin with his hair was villainously dark, and his features were unmistakable even down there in the South, and he could play chess with his eyes shut, and even then he could beat anyone in Cuba. But ther was more than this, there was the bargain he made with Bill that told one who he was. He sold that crystal for Bill Snyth's soul.

Jim Bunion leaning over the table with his breath in my face nodded his head several times and was silent.

I began to question him then. Did they play chess as far away as Cuba? He said they all did. Was it conceivable that any man would make such a bargain as Snyth made? Wasn't the trick well known? Wasn't it in hundreds of books? And if he couldn't read books mustn't he have heard from sailors that that is the Devil's commonest dodge to get souls from silly people?

Jim Bunion had leant back in his own chair quietly smiling at my questions but when I mentioned silly people he leaned forward again, and thrust his face close to mine and asked me several times if I called Bill Snyth silly. It seemed that these three sailors thought a great deal of Bill Snyth and it made Jim Bunion angry to hear anything said against him. I hastened to say that the bargain seemed silly though not of course the man who made it; for the sailor was almost threatening, and no wonder for the whiskey in that dim tavern would madden a nun.

When I said that the bargain seemed silly he smiled again, and then he thundered his fist down on the table and said that no one had ever yet got the better of Bill Snyth and that that was the worst bargain for himself that the Devil ever made, and that from all he had read or heard of the Devil he had never been so badly had before as the night when he met Bill Snyth at the inn in the thunderstorm in Cuba, for Bill Snyth already had the damnedest soul at sea; Bill was a good fellow, but his soul was damned right enough, so he got the crystal for nothing.

Yes, he was there and saw it all himself, Bill Snyth in the Spanish inn and the candles flaring, and the Devil walking in out of the rain, and then the bargain between those two old hands, and the Devil going out into the lightning, and the thunderstorm raging on, and Bill Snyth sitting chuckling to himself between the bursts of the thunder.

But I had more questions to ask and interrupted this reminiscence. Why did they
all three always play together? And a look
of something like fear came over Jim
Bunion's face; and at first he would not
speak. And then he said to me that it was
like this; they had not paid for that crystal,
but got it as their share of Jim Bunion's kit.
If they had paid for it or given something
in exchange to Bill Snyth that would have
been all right, but they couldn't do that
now because Bill was dead, and they were
not sure if the old bargain might not hold
good. And Hell must be a large and lonely
place, and to go there alone must be bad,
and so the three agreed that they would all
stick together, and use the crystal all three
or not at all, unless one died, and then the
two would use it and the one that was gone
would wait for them. And the last of the
three to go would bring the crystal with
him, or maybe the crystal would bring him.
They didn't think, he said, they were the
kind of men for Heaven, and he hoped they
knew their place better than that, but they
didn't fancy the notion of Hell alone, if Hell
it had to be. It was all right for Bill Snyth,

he was afraid of nothing. He had known perhaps five men that were not afraid of death, but Bill Snyth was not afraid of Hell. He died with a smile on his face like a child in its sleep; it was drink killed poor Bill Snyth.

This was why I had beaten Bill Sloggs; Sloggs had the crystal on him while we played, but would not use it; these sailors seemed to fear loneliness as some people fear being hurt; he was the only one of the three who could play chess at all, he had learnt it in order to be able to answer questions and keep up their pretence, but he had learnt it badly, as I found. I never saw the crystal, they never showed it to anyone; but Jim Bunion told me that night that it was about the size that the thick end of a hen's egg would be if it were round. And then he fell asleep.

There were many more questions that I would have asked him but I could not wake him up. I even pulled the table away so that he fell to the floor, but he slept on, and all the tavern was dark but for one candle burning; and it was then that I noticed for the first time that the other two sailors had gone, no one remained at all but Jim Bunion and I and the sinister barman of that curious inn, and he too was asleep.

When I saw that it was impossible to wake the sailor I went out into the night. Next day Jim Bunion would talk of it no more; and when I went back to Stavlokratz I found him already putting on paper his theory about the sailors, which became accepted by chess-players, that one of them had been taught their curious gambit and the other two between them had learnt all the defensive openings as well as general play. Though who taught them no one could say, in spite of enquiries made afterwards all along the Southern Pacific.

I never learnt any more details from any of the three sailors, they were always too drunk to speak or else not drunk enough to be communicative. I seem just to have taken Jim Bunion at the flood. But I kept my promise, it was I that introduced them to the Tournament, and a pretty mess they made of established reputations. And so they kept on for months, never losing a game and always playing for their pound a side. I used to follow them wherever they went merely to watch their play. They were more marvellous than Stavlokratz even in his youth.

But then they took to liberties such as giving their queen when playing first-class players. And in the end one day when all three were drunk they played the best player in England with only a row of pawns. They won the game all right. But the ball broke to pieces. I never smelt such a stench in all my life.

The three sailors took it stoically enough, they signed on to different ships and went back again to the sea, and the world of chess lost sight, for ever I trust, of the most remarkable players it ever knew, who would have altogether spoiled the game.

The Exile's Club

t was an evening party; and something someone had said to me had started me talking about a subject that to me is full of fascination, the subject of old religions, forsaken gods. The truth (for all religions have some of it), the wisdom, the beauty, of the religions of countries to which I travel have not the same appeal for me; for one only notices in them their tyranny and intolerance and the abject servitude that they claim from thought; but when a dynasty has been dethroned in heaven and goes forgotten and outcast even among men, one's eyes no longer dazzled by its power find something very wistful in the faces of fallen gods suppliant to be remembered, something almost tearfully beautiful, like a long warm

summer twilight fading gently away after some day memorable in the story of earthly wars. Between what Zeus, for instance, has been once and the half-remembered tale he is to-day there lies a space so great that there is no change of fortune known to man whereby we may measure the height down which he has fallen. And it is the same with many another god at whom once the ages trembled and the twentieth century treats as an old wives' tale. The fortitude that such a fall demands is surely more than human.

Some such things as these I was saying, and being upon a subject that much attracts me I possibly spoke too loudly, certainly I was not aware that standing close behind me was no less a person than the ex-King of Eritivaria, the thirty islands of the East, or I would have moderated my voice and moved away a little to give him more room. I was not aware of his presence until his satellite, one who had fallen with him into exile but still revolved about him, told me that his master desired to know me; and so to my surprise I was presented though neither of them even knew my

191

name. And that was how I came to be invited by the ex-King to dine at his club.

At the time I could only account for his wishing to know me by supposing that he found in his own exiled condition some likeness to the fallen fortunes of the gods of whom I talked unwitting of his presence; but now I know that it was not of himself he was thinking when he asked me to dine at that club.

The club would have been the most imposing building in any street in London, but in that obscure mean quarter of London in which they had built it it appeared unduly enormous. Lifting right up above those grotesque houses and built in that Greek style that we call Georgian, there was something Olympian about it. To my host an unfashionable street could have meant nothing, through all his youth wherever he had gone had become fashionable the moment he went there; words like the East End could have had no meaning to him.

Whoever built that house had enormous wealth and cared nothing for fashion, perhaps despised it. As I stood gazing at the magnificent upper windows draped with great curtains, indistinct in the evening, on which huge shadows flickered my host attracted my attention from the doorway, and so I went in and met for the second time the ex-King of Eritivaria.

In front of us a stairway of rare marble led upwards, he took me through a side-door and downstairs and we came to a banqueting-hall of great magnificence. A long table ran up the middle of it, laid for quite twenty people, and I noticed the peculiarity that instead of chairs there were thrones for everyone except me, who was the only guest and for whom there was an ordinary chair. My host explained to me when we all sat down that everyone who belonged to that club was by rights a king.

In fact none was permitted, he told me, to belong to the club until his claim to a kingdom made out in writing had been examined and allowed by those whose duty it was. The whim of a populace or the candidate's own misrule were never considered by the investigators, nothing counted with them but heredity and lawful descent from kings, all else was ignored.

At that table there were those who had once reigned themselves, others lawfully claimed descent from kings that the world had forgotten, the kingdoms claimed by some had even changed their names. Hatzgurh, the mountain kingdom, is almost regarded as mythical.

I have seldom seen greater splendour than that long hall provided below the level of the street. No doubt by day it was a little sombre, as all basements are, but at night with its great crystal chandeliers, and the glitter of heirlooms that had gone into exile, it surpassed the splendour of palaces that have only one king. They had come to London suddenly most of those kings, or their fathers before them, or forefathers; some had come away from their kingdoms by night, in a light sleigh, flogging the horses, or had galloped clear with morning over the border, some had trudged roads for days from their capital in disguise, yet many had had time just as they left to snatch up some small thing without price in markets, for the sake of old times as they said, but quite as much, I thought, with an eye to the future. And there these treasures glittered on that long table in the banqueting-hall of the basement of that strange club. Merely to see them was much, but to hear their story that their owners told was to go back in fancy to epic times on the romantic border of fable and fact, where the heroes of history fought with the gods of myth. The famous silver horses of Gilgianza were there climbing their sheer mountain, which they did by miraculous means before the time of the Goths. It was not a large piece of silver but its workmanship outrivalled the skill of the bees.

A yellow Emperor had brought out of the East a piece of that incomparable porcelain that had made his dynasty famous though all their deeds are forgotten, it had the exact shade of the right purple.

And there was a little golden statuette of a dragon stealing a diamond from a lady, the dragon had the diamond in his claws, large and of the first water. There had been a kingdom whose whole constitution and history were founded on the legend, from which alone its kings had claimed their right to the sceptre, that a dragon stole a diamond from a lady. When its last king left that country, because his favourite general used a peculiar formation under the fire of artillery, he brought with him the little ancient image that no longer proved him a king outside that singular club.

There was the pair of amethyst cups of the turbaned King of Foo, the one that he drank from himself, and the one that he gave to his enemies, eye could not tell which was which.

All these things the ex-King of Eritivaria showed me, telling me a marvellous tale of each; of his own he had brought nothing, except the mascot that used once to sit on the top of the water tube of his favourite motor.

I have not outlined a tenth of the splendour of that table, I had meant to come again and examine each piece of plate and make notes of its history; had I known that this was the last time I should wish to enter that club I should have looked at its treasures more attentively, but now as the wine went round and the exiles began to talk I took my eyes from the table and listened to strange tales of their former state.

He that has seen better times has usually

a poor tale to tell, some mean and trivial thing has been his undoing, but they that dined in that basement had mostly fallen like oaks on nights of abnormal tempest, had fallen mightily and shaken a nation. Those who had not been kings themselves, but claimed through an exiled ancestor, had stories to tell of even grander disaster, history seeming to have mellowed their dynasty's fate as moss grows over an oak a great while fallen. There were no jealousies there as so often there are among kings, rivalry must have ceased with the loss of their navies and armies, and they showed no bitterness against those that had turned them out, one speaking of the error of his Prime Minister by which he had lost his throne as "poor old Friedrich's Heaven-sent gift of tactlessness."

They gossipped pleasantly of many things, the tittle-tattle we all had to know when we were learning history, and many a wonderful story I might have heard, many a sidelight on mysterious wars had I not made use of one unfortunate word. That word was "upstairs."

The ex-King of Eritivaria having pointed

out to me those unparalleled heirlooms to which I have alluded, and many more besides, hospitably asked me if there was anything else that I would care to see, he meant the pieces of plate that they had in the cupboards, the curiously graven swords of other princes, historic jewels, legendary seals, but I who had had a glimpse of their marvellous staircase, whose balustrade I believed to be solid gold and wondering why in such a stately house they chose to dine in the basement, mentioned the word "upstairs." A profound hush came down on the whole assembly, the hush that might greet levity in a cathedral.

"Upstairs!" he gasped. "We cannot go upstairs."

I perceived that what I had said was an ill-chosen thing. I tried to excuse myself but knew not how.

"Of course," I muttered, "members may not take guests upstairs."

"Members!" he said to me. "We are not the members!"

There was such reproof in his voice that I said no more, I looked at him questioningly, perhaps my lips moved, I may have

198

said "What are you?" A great surprise had come on me at their attitude.

"We are the waiters," he said.

That I could not have known, here at least was honest ignorance that I had no need to be ashamed of, the very opulence of their table denied it.

"Then who are the members?" I asked.

Such a hush fell at that question, such a hush of genuine awe, that all of a sudden a wild thought entered my head, a thought strange and fantastic and terrible. I gripped my host by the wrist and hushed my voice.

"Are they too exiles?" I asked.

Twice as he looked in my face he gravely nodded his head.

I left that club very swiftly indeed, never to see it again, scarcely pausing to say farewell to those menial kings, and as I left the door a great window opened far up at the top of the house and a flash of lightning streamed from it and killed a dog.

The Three Infernal Jokes

his is the story that the desolate man told to me on the lonely Highland road one autumn evening with winter coming on and the stags roaring.

The saddening twilight, the mountain already black, the dreadful melancholy of the stags' voices, his friendless mournful face, all seemed to be of some most sorrowful play staged in that valley by an outcast god, a lonely play of which the hills were part and he the only actor.

For long we watched each other drawing out of the solitudes of those forsaken spaces. Then when we met he spoke.

"I will tell you a thing that will make you die of laughter. I will keep it to myself no longer. But first I must tell you how I came by it."

I do not give the story in his words with all his woeful interjections and the misery of his frantic self-reproaches for I would not convey unnecessarily to my readers that atmosphere of sadness that was about all he said and that seemed to go with him wherever he moved.

It seems that he had been a member of a club, a West-end club he called it, a respectable but quite inferior affair, probably in the City: agents belonged to it, fire insurance mostly, but life insurance and motor-agents too, it was in fact a touts' club.

It seems that a few of them one evening, forgetting for a moment their encyclopedias and non-stop tyres, were talking loudly over a card-table when the game had ended about their personal virtues, and a very little man with waxed moustaches who disliked the taste of wine was boasting heartily of his temperance. It was then that he who told this mournful story, drawn on by the boasts of others, leaned forward a little over the green baize into the light of the two guttering candles and revealed, no doubt a little shyly, his own extraordinary virtue. One woman was to him as ugly as another.

And the silenced boasters rose and went home to bed leaving him all alone, as he supposed, with his unequalled virtue. And yet he was not alone, for when the rest had gone there arose a member out of a deep arm-chair at the dark end of the room and walked across to him, a man whose occupation he did not know and only now suspects.

"You have," said the stranger, "a surpassing virtue."

"I have no possible use for it," my poor friend replied.

"Then doubtless you would sell it cheap," said the stranger.

Something in the man's manner or appearance made the desolate teller of this mournful tale feel his own inferiority, which probably made him feel acutely shy, so that his mind abased itself as an Oriental does his body in the presence of a superior, or perhaps he was sleepy, or merely a little drunk. Whatever it was he only mumbled, " O yes," instead of contradicting so mad a remark. And the stranger led the way to the room where the telephone was.

"I think you will find my firm will give a good price for it," he said: and without more ado he began with a pair of pincers to cut the wire of the telephone and the receiver. The old waiter who looked after the club they had left shuffling round the other room putting things away for the night.

"Whatever are you doing of?" said my friend.

"This way," said the stranger. Along a passage they went and away to the back of the club and there the stranger leaned out of a window and fastened the severed wires to the lightning conductor. My friend has no doubt of that, a broad ribbon of copper, half an inch wide, perhaps wider, running down from the roof to the earth.

"Hell," said the stranger with his mouth to the telephone; then silence for a while with his ear to the receiver, leaning out of the window. And then my friend heard his poor virtue being several times repeated, and then words like Yes and No.

"They offer you three jokes," said the stranger, "which shall make all who hear them simply die of laughter."

I think my friend was reluctant then to have anything more to do with it, he wanted to go home; he said he didn't want jokes.

"They think very highly of your virtue," said the stranger. And at that, odd as it seems, my friend wavered, for logically if they thought highly of the goods they should have paid a higher price.

"O all right," he said.

The extraordinary document that the agent drew from his pocket ran something like this:

"I . . . . . in consideration of three new jokes received from Mr. Montagu-Montague, hereinafter to be called the agent, and warranted to be as by him stated and described, do assign to him, yield, abrogate and give up all recognitions, emoluments, perquisites or rewards due to me Here or Elsewhere on account of the following virtue, to wit and that is to say . . . . . that all women are to me equally ugly." The last eight words being filled in in ink by Mr. Montagu-Montague.

My poor friend duly signed it. "These are the jokes," said the agent. They were boldly written on three slips of paper.

"They don't seem very funny," said the other when he had read them. "You are immune," said Mr. Montagu-Montague, "but anyone else who hears them will simply die of laughter: that we guarantee."

An American firm had bought at the price of waste paper a hundred thousand copies of The Dictionary of Electricity written when electricity was new, — and it had turned out that even at the time its author had not rightly grasped his subject, — the firm had paid £10,000 to a respectable English paper (no other in fact than the Briton) for the use of its name, and to obtain orders for The Briton Dictionary of Electricity was the occupation of my unfortunate friend. He seems to have had a way with him. Apparently he knew by a glance at a man, or a look round at his garden, whether to recommend the book as "an absolutely up-to-date achievement, the finest thing of its kind in the world of modern science" or as "at once quaint and imperfect, a thing to buy and to keep as a tribute to those dear old times that are gone." So he went on with this quaint though usual business, putting aside the memory of that night as an occasion on which he had "somewhat exceeded" as they say in circles where a spade is called neither a spade nor an agricultural implement but is never mentioned at all, being altogether too vulgar.

And then one night he put on his suit of dress clothes and found the three jokes in the pocket. That was perhaps a shock. He seems to have thought it over carefully then, and the end of it was he gave a dinner at the club to twenty of the members. The dinner would do no harm he thought — might even help the business, and if the joke came off he would be a witty fellow, and two jokes still up his sleeve.

Whom he invited or how the dinner went I do not know for he began to speak rapidly and came straight to the point, as a stick that nears a cataract suddenly goes faster and faster. The dinner was duly served, the port went round, the twenty men were smoking, two waiters loitered, when he after carefully reading the best of the jokes told it down the table. They laughed. One man accidentally inhaled his cigar smoke and spluttered, the two waiters overheard and tittered behind their hands, one man, a bit of a raconteur himself, quite clearly wished not to laugh, but his veins swelled dangerously in trying to keep it back, and in the end he laughed too. The joke had succeeded; my friend smiled at the thought; he wished to say little deprecating things to the man on his right; but the laughter did not stop and the waiters would not be silent. He waited, and waited wondering; the laughter went roaring on, distinctly louder now, and the waiters as loud as any. It had gone on for three or four minutes when this frightful thought leaped up all at once in his mind: *it was forced laughter!* However could anything have induced him to tell so foolish a joke? He saw its absurdity as in revelation; and the more he thought of it as these people laughed at him, even the waiters too, the more he felt that he could never lift up his head with his brother touts again. And still the laughter went roaring and choking on. He was very angry. There was not much use in having a friend, he thought, if one silly joke could not be overlooked; he had fed them too. And then he felt that he had no friends at all, and his anger faded away, and a great unhappiness came down on him, and he got quietly up and slunk from the room and slipped away from the club. Poor man, he scarcely had the heart next morning even to glance at the papers, but you did not need to glance at them, big type was bandied about that day as though it were common type, the words of the headlines stared at you; and the headlines said:— Twenty-Two Dead Men at a Club.

Yes, he saw it then: the laughter had not stopped, some had probably burst blood vessels, some must have choked, some succumbed to nausea, heart-failure must have mercifully taken some, and they were his friends after all, and none had escaped, not even the waiters. It was that infernal joke.

He thought out swiftly, and remembers clear as a nightmare, the drive to Victoria Station, the boat-train to Dover and going disguised to the boat: and on the boat pleasantly smiling, almost obsequious, two constables that wished to speak for a moment with Mr. Watkyn-Jones. That was his name.

In a third-class carriage with handcuffs on his wrists, with forced conversation when any, he returned between his captors to Victoria to be tried for murder at the High Court of Bow.

At the trial he was defended by a young barrister of considerable ability who had gone into the Cabinet in order to enhance his forensic reputation. And he was ably defended. It is no exaggeration to say that the speech for the defence showed it to be usual, even natural and right, to give a dinner to twenty men and to slip away without ever saying a word, leaving all, with the waiters, dead. That was the impression left in the minds of the jury. And Mr. Watkyn-Jones felt himself practically free, with all the advantages of his awful experience, and his two jokes intact. But lawyers are still experimenting with the new act which allows a prisoner to give evidence. They do not like to make no use of it for fear they may be thought not to know of the act, and a lawyer who is not in touch with the very latest laws is soon regarded as not being up to date and he may drop as much as £50,000 a year in fees. And therefore though it always hangs their clients they hardly like to neglect it.

Mr. Watkyn-Jones was put in the witness box. There he told the simple truth, and a very poor affair it seemed after the impassioned and beautiful things that were uttered by the counsel for the defence. Men and women had wept when they heard that. They did not weep when they heard Watkyn-Jones. Some tittered. It no longer seemed a right and natural thing to leave one's guests all dead and to fly the country. Where was Justice, they asked, if anyone could do that? And when his story was told the judge rather happily asked if he could make him die of laughter too. And what was the joke? For in so grave a place as a Court of Justice no fatal effects need be feared. And hesitatingly the prisoner pulled from his pocket the three slips of paper: and perceived for the first time that the one on which the first and best joke had been written had become quite blank. Yet he could remember it, and only too clearly. And he told it from memory to the Court.

"An Irishman once on being asked by his master to buy a morning paper said in his usual witty way, 'Arrah and begorrah and

210

I will be after wishing you the top of the morning.'"

No joke sounds quite so good the second time it is told, it seems to lose something of its essence, but Watkyn-Jones was not prepared for the awful stillness with which this one was received; nobody smiled; and it had killed twenty-two men. The joke was bad, devilish bad; counsel for the defence was frowning, and an usher was looking in a little bag for something the judge wanted. And at this moment, as though from far away, without his wishing it, there entered the prisoner's head, and shone there and would not go, this old bad proverb: "As well be hung for a sheep as for a lamb." The jury seemed to be just about to retire. "I have another joke," said Watkyn-Jones, and then and there he read from the second slip of paper. He watched the paper curiously to see if it would go blank, occupying his mind with so slight a thing as men in dire distress very often do, and the words were almost immediately expunged, swept swiftly as if by a hand, and he saw the paper before him as blank as the first. And they were laughing this time, judge, jury, counsel for the prosecution, audience and all, and the grim men that watched him upon either side. There was no mistake about this joke.

He did not stay to see the end, and walked out with his eyes fixed on the ground, unable to bear a glance to the right or left. And since then he has wandered, avoiding ports and roaming lonely places. Two years have known him on the Highland roads, often hungry, always friendless, always changing his district, wandering lonely on with his deadly joke.

Sometimes for a moment he will enter inns, driven by cold and hunger, and hear men in the evening telling jokes and even challenging him; but he sits desolate and silent, lest his only weapon should escape from him and his last joke spread mourning in a hundred cots. His beard has grown and turned grey and is mixed with moss and weeds, so that no one, I think, not even the police, would recognise him now for that dapper tout that sold The Briton Dictionary of Electricity in such a different land.

He paused, his story told, and then his lip quivered as though he would say more, and I believe he intended then and there to yield up his deadly joke on that Highland road and to go forth then with his three blank slips of paper, perhaps to a felon's cell, with one more murder added to his crimes, but harmless at last to man. I therefore hurried on, and only heard him mumbling sadly behind me, standing bowed and broken, all alone in the twilight, perhaps telling over and over even then the last infernal joke.

THE END

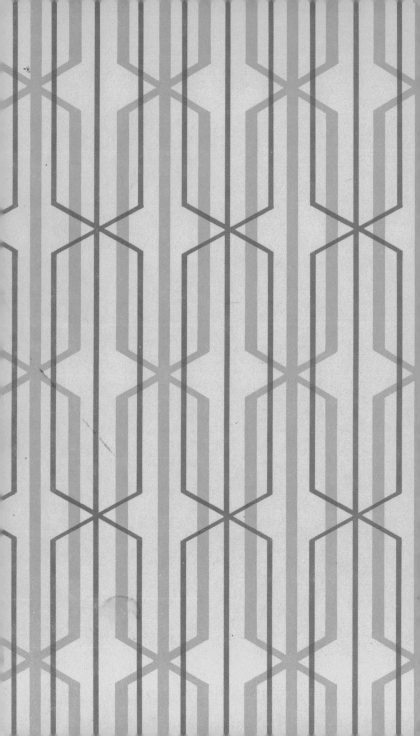